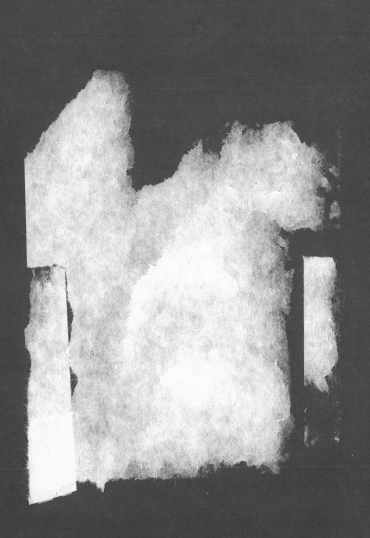

THE LEOPARD HUNTS IN DARKNESS

Novels by Wilbur Smith

THE
LEOPARD
HUNTS
IN
DARKNESS

•

Wilbur Smith

DOUBLEDAY & COMPANY, INC.
GARDEN CITY, NEW YORK   1984

THE LEOPARD HUNTS IN DARKNESS was originally
published in Great Britain by William Heinemann Ltd.

Library of Congress Cataloging in Publication Data

Smith, Wilbur A.
The leopard hunts in darkness.

I. Title.
PR9405.9.S5L4   1984   823   84–4078
ISBN 0-385-18737-8

For Danielle,
with all my love

THE LEOPARD HUNTS IN DARKNESS

THIS small wind had travelled a thousand miles and more, up from the great wastes of the Kalahari Desert which the little yellow Bushmen call the "Big Dry." Now when it reached the escarpment of the Zambezi valley, it broke up into eddies and backlashes among the hills and the broken ground of the rim.

The bull elephant stood just below the crest of one of the hills, much too canny to silhouette himself on the skyline. His bulk was screened by the new growth of leaves on the msasa trees, and he blended with the grey rock of the slope behind him.

He reached up twenty feet and sucked the air into his wide, hair-rimmed nostrils, and then he rolled his trunk down and delicately blew into his own gaping mouth. The two olfactory organs in the overhang of his upper lip flared open like pink rosebuds, and he tasted the air.

He tasted the fine peppery dust of the far deserts, the sweet pollens of a hundred wild plants, the warm bovine stench of the buffalo herd in the valley below, the cool tang of the water pool at which they were drinking and wallowing; these and other scents he identified, and accurately he judged the proximity of the source of each odour.

However, these were not the scents for which he was searching. What he sought was the other acrid offensive smell which overlaid all the others. The smell of native tobacco smoke mingled with the peculiar musk of the flesh-eater, rancid sweat in unwashed wool, of paraffin and carbolic soap and cured leather—the scent of man; it was there, as strong and close as it had been in all the long days since the chase had begun.

Once again the old bull felt the atavistic rage rising in him. Countless generations of his kind had been pursued by that odour. Since a calf, he had learned to hate and fear it, almost all his life he had been driven by it.

Only recently there had been a hiatus in the lifelong pursuit and flight. For eleven years there had been surcease, a time of quiet for the herds along the Zambezi. The bull could not know or understand the reason, that there had been bitter civil war among his tormentors, war that had turned these vast areas along the south bank of the Zambezi into an undefended buffer zone, too dangerous for ivory-hunters or even for the game rangers whose duties included the culling of surplus elephant populations. The herds had prospered in those years, but now the persecution had begun again with all the old implacable ferocity.

With the rage and the terror still upon him, the old bull lifted his trunk again and sucked the dreaded scent into the sinuses of his bony skull. Then he turned and, moving silently, he crossed the rocky ridge, a mere greyish blur for an instant against the clear blue of the African sky. Still carrying the scent, he strode down to where his herd was spread along the back slope.

There were almost three hundred elephants scattered among the trees. Most of the breeding cows had calves with them, some so young that they looked like fat little piglets, small enough to fit under their mothers' bellies. They rolled up their tiny trunks onto their foreheads and craned upwards to the teats that hung on swollen dugs between the dams' front legs.

The older calves cavorted about, romping and playing noisy tag, until in exasperation one of their elders would tear a branch from one of the trees and, wielding it in his trunk, lay about him, scattering the importunate youngsters in squealing, mock consternation.

The cows and young bulls fed with unhurried deliberation, working a trunk deep into a dense, fiercely thorned thicket to pluck a handful of ripe berries and then place them well back in the throat like an old man swallowing aspirin; or using the point of a stained ivory tusk to loosen the bark of a msasa tree and then strip ten feet of it and stuff it happily beyond the drooping triangular lower lip; or raising their entire bulk on their back legs like a begging dog to reach up with outstretched trunk to the tender leaves at the top of a tall tree, or using a broad forehead and four tons of weight to shake another tree until it tossed and whipped and released a shower of ripe pods. Farther down the slope two young bulls had combined their strength to topple a sixty-footer whose top leaves were beyond even their long reach. As it fell with a crackle of tearing fibres, the herd bull crossed the ridge and immediately the happy uproar ceased, to be replaced by quiet that was startling in its contrast.

The calves pressed anxiously to their mothers' flanks, and the grown beasts froze defensively, ears outstretched and only the tips of their trunks questing.

The bull came down to them with swinging stride, carrying his thick yellow ivories high, his alarm evident in the cock of his tattered ears.

He was still carrying the man-smell in his head, and when he reached the nearest group of cows, he extended his trunk and blew it over them.

Instantly they spun away, instinctively turning downwind so that the pursuers' scent must always be carried to them. The rest of the herd saw the manoeuvre and fell into their running formation, closing up with the calves and nursing mothers in the centre, the old barren queens surrounding them, the young bulls pointing the herd and the older bulls and their attendant askaris on the flanks; and they went away in the ground-devouring stride that they could maintain for a day and a night and another day without check.

As he fled, the old bull was confused. No pursuit he had ever experienced was as persistent as this. It had lasted for eight days now, and yet the pursuers never closed in to make contact with the herd. They were in the south, giving him their scent, but almost always keeping beyond the limited range of his weak eyesight. There seemed to be many of them, more than he had ever encountered in all his wanderings, a line stretched like a net across the southern routes. Only once had he seen them. On the fifth day, having reached the limits of forbearance, he had turned the herd and tried to break back through their line, and they had been there to head him off, the tiny upright sticklike figures, so deceptively frail and yet so deadly, springing up from the yellow grass, barring his escape to the south, flapping blankets and beating on empty paraffin tins, until his courage failed and the old bull turned back, and led his herds once more down the rugged escarpment towards the great river.

The escarpment was threaded by elephant trails used for ten thousand years, trails that followed the easier gradients and found the passes and ports through the ironstone ramparts. The old bull worked his herd down one of these, and the herd strung out in single file through the narrow places and spread out again beyond.

He kept them going through the night. Though there was no moon, the fat white stars hung close against the earth, and the herd moved almost soundlessly through the dark forests. Once, after midnight, the old bull fell back and waited beside the trail, letting his herd go on. Within the hour he caught again the tainted man-smell on the wind, fainter and very much more distant—but there, always there, and he hurried forward to catch up with his cows.

In the dawn they entered the area which he had not visited in ten years. The narrow strip along the river had been the scene of intense human activity during the long-drawn-out war, and which for that reason he had avoided until now when he was reluctantly driven into it once again.

The herd moved with less urgency. They had left the pursuit far behind, and they slowed so that they could feed as they went. The forest was greener and more lush here on the bottom lands of the valley. The msasa forests had given way to mopani and giant swollen baobabs that flourished in the heat, and the old bull could sense the water ahead and he rumbled thirstily deep in his belly. Yet some instinct warned him of other danger ahead as well as behind. He paused often, swinging his great grey head slowly from side to side, his ears held out like sounding boards, his small weak eyes gleaming as he searched cautiously before moving on again.

Then abruptly he stopped once more. Something at the limit of his vision had caught his attention, something that glistened metallically in the slanted morning sunlight. He flared back with alarm, and behind him his herd backed up, his fear transmitted to them infectiously.

The bull stared at the speck of reflected light, and slowly his alarm receded, for there was no movement except the soft passage of the breeze through the forest, no sound but the whisper of it in the branches and the lulling chattering and hum of unconcerned bird and insect life around him. Still the old bull waited, staring ahead, and as the light altered he noticed there were other identical metal objects in a line across his front, and he shifted his weight from one forefoot to the other, making a little fluttering sound of indecision in his throat.

What had alarmed the old bull was a line of small square galvanized sheet-metal plaques. They were each affixed to the top of an iron dropper that had been hammered into the earth so many years ago that all man-smell had long ago dissipated. On each plaque was painted a laconic warning, which had faded in the brutal sunlight from crimson to pale pink, a stylized skull and crossbones above the words, "DANGER. MINEFIELD."

The minefield had been laid years previously by the security forces of the now-defunct white Rhodesian government, as a *cordon sanitaire* along the Zambezi River, an attempt to prevent the guerrilla forces of ZIPRA and ZAPU from entering the territory from their bases across the river in Zambia. Millions of anti-personnel mines and heavier Claymores made up a continuous field so long and deep that it would never be cleared; the cost of doing so would be prohibitive to the country's new black government already in serious economic difficulties.

While the old bull still hesitated, the air became filled with a clattering roar, the wild sound of hurricane winds. The sound came from behind the herd, from the south again, and the old bull swung away from the minefield to face it.

Low over the forest tops rushed a grotesque dark shape, suspended on a whistling silver disc. Filling the sky with noise, it bore down upon the bunched herd, so low that the down-draught from its spinning rotor churned the branches of the tree-tops into thrashing confusion and flung up a fog of red dust from the earth's dry surface.

Driven by this new menace, the old bull turned and rushed forward beyond the sparse line of metal discs and his terror-stricken herd charged after him into the minefield.

He was fifty metres into the field before the first mine exploded under him. It burst upwards into the thick leather pad of his right hind foot, cutting half of it away like an axe-stroke. Raw red meat hung in tatters from it and white bone gleamed deep in the wound as the bull lurched forward on three legs. The next mine hit him squarely in the right fore, and smashed his foot into bloody mince to the ankle. The bull squealed in agony and panic and fell back on his haunches pinned by his shattered limbs, while all around him his breeding herd ran on into the minefield.

The thump, thump of detonations was intermittent at first, strung out along the edge of the field, but soon they took on a broken staccato beat like that of a maniac drummer. Occasionally four or five mines exploded simultaneously, an intense blurt of sound that struck the hills of the escarpment and shattered into a hundred echoes.

Underlying it all, like the string section of some hellish orchestra, was the whistling clatter of the helicopter rotor as the machine dipped and swung and dropped and rose along the periphery of the minefield, worrying the milling herd like a sheepdog its flock, darting here to head off a bunch of animals that had broken back, racing there to catch a fine young bull who had miraculously run unscathed through the field and reached the clear ground of the river-bank, settling in his path, forcing him to stop and turn, then chasing him back into the minefield until a mine tore his foot away and he went down trumpeting and screaming.

Now the thunder of bursting mines was as continuous as a naval bombardment, and each explosion threw a column of dust high into the still air of the valley, so that the red fog cloaked some of the horror of it. The dust twisted and eddied as high as the tree-tops and transformed the frenzied animals to tormented wraiths lit by the flashes of the bursting mines.

One old cow with all four feet blown away lay upon her side and flogged her head against the hard earth in her attempts to rise. Another dragged herself forward on her belly, back legs trailing, her trunk flung protectively over the tiny calf beside her until a Claymore went off under her chest and burst her ribs outwards like the staves of a barrel, at the same instant tearing away the hindquarters of the calf at her side.

Other calves, separated from their dams, rushed squealing through the dust fog, ears flattened against their heads in terror, until a clap of sound and a flash of brief fire bowled them over in a tangle of shattered limbs.

It went on for a long time, and then the barrage of explosions slowed, became intermittent once more, and gradually ceased. The helicopter settled to earth, beyond the line of warning markers. The beat of its engine died, and the spinning rotor stilled. The only sound now was the screaming of the maimed and dying beasts lying in the churned earth below the dust-coated trees. The hatch of the helicopter was open and a man dropped lightly from it to the earth.

He was dressed in a faded denim jacket from which the sleeves had been carefully removed, and tight-fitting tie-dyed jeans. In the days of the Rhodesian war, denim had been the unofficial uniform of the guerrilla fighters. On his feet he wore fancy, tooled, western boots, and pushed up on the top of his head gold-rimmed Polaroid aviator's sunglasses. These and the row of ball-point pens clipped into the breast-pocket of his jacket were badges of rank among the veteran guerrillas. Under his right arm he carried an AK 47 assault rifle, as he walked to the edge of the minefield and stood for a full five minutes impassively watching the carnage lying out there in the forest. Then the black man walked back towards the helicopter.

Behind the canopy, the pilot's face was turned attentively towards him, with his earphones still in place over his elaborate Afro-style hairdo, but the officer ignored him and concentrated instead on the machine's fuselage.

All the insignia and identification numbers had been carefully covered with masking tape, and oversprayed with black enamel from a hand-held aerosol can. In one place the tape had come loose, exposing a corner of the identification lettering. The officer pressed it back into place with the heel of his hand, inspected his work briefly but critically, and turned away to the shade of the nearest mopani.

He propped his AK 47 against the trunk, spread a handkerchief upon the earth to protect his jeans and sat down with his back to the rough bark. He lit a cigarette with a gold Dunhill lighter and inhaled deeply, before letting the smoke trickle gently over his lips.

Then he smiled for the first time, a cool reflective smile, as he considered how many men, and how much time and ammunition it would take to kill three hundred elephant in the conventional manner.

"The comrade commissar has lost none of his cunning from the old days of the bush war—who else would have thought of this?" He shook his head in admiration and respect.

When he had finished the cigarette, he crushed the butt to powder between his thumb and forefinger, a little habit from those far-off days, and closed his eyes.

The terrible chorus of groans and screams from the minefield could not keep him from sleep. Later, it was the sound of men's voices that woke him. He stood up quickly, instantly alert, and glanced at the sun. Past noon.

He went to the helicopter and woke the pilot.

"They are coming."

He took the loud hailer from its clamp on the bulkhead and waited in the open hatchway until the first of them came out from among the trees, and he looked at them with amused contempt.

"Baboons!" he murmured, with the contempt of the educated man for the peasant, of one African for another of a different tribe.

They came in a long file, following the elephant trail. Two or three hundred, dressed in animal-skin cloaks and ragged western cast-offs, the men leading and the women bringing up the rear. Many of the women were bare-breasted, and some of them were young with a saucy tilt to the head and a lyrical swing of round buttocks under brief animal-tail kilts. As the denim-clad officer watched them, his contempt changed to appreciation: perhaps he would find time for one of them later, he thought, and put his hand into the pocket of his jeans at the thought. They lined the edge of the minefield, jabbering and screeching with delight, some of them capering and giggling and pointing out to each other the masses of stricken beasts.

The officer let them vent their glee. They had earned this pause for self-congratulation. They had been eight days on the trail, almost without rest, acting in shifts as beaters to drive the elephant herd down the escarpment. While he waited for them to quieten, he considered again the personal magnetism and force of character that could weld this mob of primitive illiterate peasants into a cohesive and effective whole. One man had engineered the entire operation.

"He is a man!" the officer nodded, then roused himself from the indulgence of hero-worship and lifted the trumpet of the loud hailer to his lips.

"Be quiet! Silence!" He stilled them, and began to allocate the work that must be done.

He picked the butcher gangs from those who were armed with axe and panga. He set the women to building the smoking racks and plaiting baskets of mopani bark, others he ordered to gather wood for the fires. Then he turned his attention back to the butchers.

None of the tribesmen had ever ridden in an aircraft and the officer had to use the pointed toe of his western boot to persuade the first of them to climb into the hatch for the short hop over the mine-sown strip to the nearest carcass.

Leaning out of the hatchway, the officer peered down at the old bull. He appraised the thick curved ivory, and then saw that the beast had bled to death during the waiting hours, and he signalled the pilot lower.

He placed his lips close to the eldest tribesman's ear.

"Let not your feet touch the earth, on your life!" he shouted, and the man nodded jerkily. "The tusks first, then the meat."

The man nodded again.

The officer slapped his shoulder and the elder jumped down onto the bull's belly that was already swelling with fermenting gases. He balanced agilely upon it. The rest of his gang, clutching their axes, followed him down.

At the officer's hand signal the helicopter rose and darted like a dragonfly to the next animal that showed good ivory from the lip. This one was still alive, and heaved itself into a sitting position, reaching up with bloody dust-smeared trunk to try and pluck the hovering helicopter from the air.

Braced in the hatch, the officer sighted down the AK 47 and fired a single shot into the back of the neck where it joined the skull, and the cow collapsed and lay as still as the body of her calf beside her. The officer nodded at the leader of the next gang of butchers.

Balanced on the gigantic grey heads, careful not to let a foot touch the earth, the axemen chipped the tusks loose from their castles of white bone. It was delicate work, for a careless stroke could drastically diminish the value of the ivory. They had seen the officer in tie-dyed jeans, with a short, well-timed swing of the rifle-butt, break the jaw of a man who merely queried an order. What would he do with one who ruined a tusk? They worked with care. As the tusks were freed, the helicopter winched them up and then carried the gang to the next carcass.

By nightfall most of the elephant had died of their massive wounds or had been shot to death, but the screams of those who had not yet received the *coup de grâce* mingled with the hubbub of the gathering jackal and hyena packs to make the night hideous. The axemen worked on by the light of grass torches, and by the first light of dawn all the ivory had been gathered in.

Now the axemen could turn their attention to butchering and dis-membering the carcasses. The rising heat worked more swiftly than they could. The stench of putrefying flesh mingled with the gases from ruptured entrails and drove the skulking scavengers to fresh paroxysms of gluttonous anticipation. The helicopter carried each haunch or shoulder as it was hacked free to the safe ground beyond the minefield. The women cut the meat into strips and festooned it on the smoking racks above the smouldering fires of green wood.

While he supervised the work, the officer was calculating the spoils. It was a pity they could not save the hides, for each was worth a thousand dollars, but they were too bulky and could not be sufficiently preserved. Putrefaction would render them worthless. On the other hand, mild putrefaction would give the meat more zest on the African palate—in the same way that an Englishman enjoys his game high.

Five hundred tons of wet meat would lose half its weight in the drying process, but the copper mines of neighbouring Zambia, with tens of thousands of labourers to feed, were eager markets for proteins. Two dollars a pound for the crudely smoked meat was the price that had already been agreed. That was a million U.S. dollars—and then of course there was the ivory.

The ivory had been ferried by the helicopter half a mile beyond the sprawling camp to a secluded place in the hills. There it had been laid out in rows, and a selected gang set to work removing the fat white cone-shaped nerve mass from the hollow end of each tusk and cleansing the ivory of any blood and muck that might betray it to the sensitive nose of an oriental customs officer.

There were four hundred tusks. Some of those taken from immature animals weighed only a few pounds, but the old bull's tusks would go well over eighty pounds apiece. A good average was twenty pounds over the lot. The going price in Hong Kong was a hundred dollars a pound, or a total of eight hundred thousand dollars. The profit on the day's work would be over one million dollars, in a land where the average annual income of each adult male was less than six hundred dollars.

Of course, there had been the other small costs of the operation. One of the axemen had overbalanced and tumbled from his perch on an elephant carcass. He had landed flat on his buttocks, directly on top of an anti-personnel mine.

"Son of a demented baboon." The officer was still irritated by the man's stupidity. It had held work up for almost an hour while the body was retrieved and prepared for burial.

Another man had lost a foot from an overzealous axe-stroke, and a dozen others had lesser cuts from swinging pangas. One other man had died during the night with an AK 47 bullet through the belly when he objected to what the officer was doing to his junior wife in the bushes beyond the smoking racks—but when the profit was considered, the costs were small indeed. The comrade commissar would be pleased, and with good reason.

It was the morning of the third day before the team working on the ivory had completed their task to the officer's satisfaction. Then they were sent down the valley to assist at the smoking racks, leaving the ivory camp deserted. There must be no eyes to discover the identity of the important visitor who would come now to inspect the spoils.

He arrived in the helicopter. The officer was standing to attention in the clearing beside the long rows of gleaming ivory. The down-draught of the rotor tore at his jacket, and fluttered the legs of his jeans, but he maintained his rigid stance.

The machine settled to earth and a commanding figure stepped down, a handsome man, straight and strong, with very white square teeth against the dark mahogany of his face, crisp kinky African hair cropped closely to the finely shaped skull. He wore an expensive pearl-grey suit of Italian cut over a white shirt and dark blue tie. His black shoes were handmade of soft calf.

He held out his hand towards the officer. Immediately the younger man abandoned his respectful pose and ran to him, like a child to its father.

"Comrade Commissar!"

"No! No!" he chided the officer gently, still smiling. "Not Comrade Commissar any longer, but Comrade Minister now. No longer leader of a bunch of unwashed bush fighters, but Minister of State of a sovereign government." The minister permitted himself a smile as he surveyed the rows of fresh tusks. "And the most successful ivory-poacher of all time—is that not true?"

*   *   *

Craig Mellow winced as the cab hit another pothole in the surface of Fifth Avenue just outside the entrance to Bergdorf Goodman. Like most New York cabs, its suspension would have better suited a Sherman tank.

"I've had a softer ride through the Mbabwe depression in a Land-Rover," Craig thought, and had a sudden nostalgic twinge as he remembered that rutted, tortuous track through the bad lands below the Chobe River, that wide green tributary of the great Zambezi.

That was all so far away and long ago, and he pushed the memory aside and returned to brooding over the sense of slight that he felt at having to ride in a yellow cab to a luncheon meeting with his publisher, and having to pick up the tab for the ride himself. There had been a time when they would have sent a chauffeur-driven limousine for him, and the destination would have been the Four Seasons or La Grenouille, not some pasta joint in the Village. Publishers made these subtle little protests when a writer had not delivered a manuscript for three years and spent more time romancing his stockbroker and living it up at Studio 54 than at his typewriter.

"Well, I guess I've got it coming." Craig made a face, reached for a cigarette, and then arrested the movement as he remembered that he had given them up. Instead he pushed the thick lock of hair off his forehead and watched the faces of the crowds on the sidewalk. There had been a time when he found the bustle exciting and stimulating after the silences of the African bush; even the sleazy façades and neon frontings onto the littered streets had been different and intriguing. Now he felt suffocated and claustrophobic, and he longed for a glimpse of open sky, rather than that narrow ribbon that showed between the high tops of the buildings.

The cab braked sharply, interrupting his thoughts, and the driver muttered "Sixteenth Street" without looking round.

Craig pushed a ten-dollar bill through the slot in the armoured Perspex screen that protected the driver from his passengers. "Keep it," he said, and stepped out onto the sidewalk. He saw the restaurant immediately, all cutesy ethnic awnings and straw-covered Chianti bottles in the window.

When Craig crossed the sidewalk he moved easily, without trace of a limp, so that nobody watching him would have guessed at his disability. Despite his misgivings, it was cool and clean inside the restaurant and the smell of food was appetizing.

Ashe Levy stood up from a booth at the back of the room and beckoned to him.

"Craig, baby!" He put one arm around Craig's shoulders and patted his cheek paternally. "You're looking good, you old hound dog, you!"

Ashe cultivated his own eclectic style. His hair was brush-cut and he wore gold-rimmed spectacles. His shirt was striped with a contrasting white collar, platinum cuff-links and tie-pin, and brown brogues with a pattern of little holes punched in the toe-caps. His jacket was cashmere with narrow lapels. His eyes were very pale, and always focused just a little to one side of Craig's own. Craig knew that he smoked only the very best Tijuana gold.

"Nice place, Ashe. How did you find it?"

"A change from the boring old 'Seasons.'" Ashe grinned slyly, pleased that the gesture of disapproval had been noted. "Craig, I want you to meet a very talented lady."

She had been sitting well back in the gloom at the back of the booth, but now she leaned forward and held out her hand. The spotlamp caught the hand, and so it was the first impression that Craig had of her.

The hand was narrow with artistic fingers, the nails were scrubbed clean, although they were clipped short and unpainted, the skin was tanned to gold with prominent aristocratic veins showing bluish beneath it. The bones were fine, but there were callouses at the base of those long straight fingers—a hand that was accustomed to hard work.

Craig took the hand and felt the strength of it, the softness of the dry cool skin on the back and the rough places on the palm, and he looked into her face.

She had thick eyebrows that stretched in an unbroken curve from the outer corner of one eye to the other. Her eyes, even in the poor light, were green with honey-coloured specks surrounding the pupil. Their gaze was direct and candid.

"Sally-Anne Jay," Ashe said. "This is Craig Mellow."

The nose was straight but slightly too large, and the mouth too wide to be beautiful. Her thick dark hair was pulled back severely from the broad forehead, her face was as honey-tanned as her hands and there was a fine peppering of freckles across her cheeks.

"I read your book," she said. Her voice was level and clear, her accent mid-Atlantic, but only when he heard its timbre did he realize how young she was. "I thought it deserved everything that happened to it."

"Compliment or slap?" He tried to make it sound light and unconcerned, but he found himself hoping fervently that she was not one of those who attempted to demonstrate their own exalted literary standards by denigrating a popular writer's work to his face.

"Very good things happened to it," she pointed out, and Craig felt absurdly pleased, even though that seemed to be the end of that topic as far as she was concerned. To show his pleasure he held her hand a little longer than was necessary, and she took it back from him and replaced it firmly in her lap.

So she wasn't a scalp-hunter, and she wasn't going to gush. Anyway, he told himself, he was bored with literary groupies trying to storm his bed, and gushers were as bad as knockers—almost.

"Let's see if we can get Ashe to buy us a drink," he suggested, and slipped into the booth facing her across the table.

Ashe made his usual fuss over the wine list, but they ended up with a ten-dollar Frascati after all.

"Nice smooth fruit." Ashe rolled it on his tongue.

"It's cold and wet," Craig said, and Ashe smiled again as they both remembered the '70 Corton-Charlemagne they had drunk the last time.

"We are expecting another guest later," Ashe told the waiter. "We'll order then." And turning to Craig, "I wanted an opportunity for Sally-Anne to show you her stuff."

"Show me," Craig invited, immediately defensive once again. The woods were full of them, the ones who wanted to ride on his strike—with unpublished manuscripts for him to endorse, investment advisers who would look after all those lovely royalties for him, others who would allow him to write their life stories and generously split the profits with him or sell him insurance or a South Sea Island paradise, commission him to write movie scripts for a small advance and an even smaller slice of any profits, all kinds gathering like hyenas to the lion's kill.

Sally-Anne lifted a portfolio from the floor beside her and placed it on the table in front of Craig. While Ashe adjusted the spotlight, she untied the ribbons that secured the folder and sat back.

Craig opened the cover and went very still. He felt the goose bumps rise along his forearms, and the hair at the nape of his neck prickle—

this was his reaction to greatness, to anything perfectly beautiful. There was a Gauguin in the Metropolitan Museum on Central Park—a Polynesian madonna carrying the Christ child on her shoulder. She had made his hair prickle. There were passages of T. S. Eliot's poetry and of Lawrence Durrell's prose that made his hair prickle every time he read them.

The opening bar of Beethoven's Fifth Symphony, those incredible *jeté* leaps of Rudolf Nureyev, and the way Nicklaus and Borg struck the ball on their good days—those things had made him prickle, and now this girl was doing it to him also.

It was a photograph. The finish was eggshell grain so every detail was crisp, the colours clear and perfectly true.

The photograph was of an elephant, an old bull. He faced the camera in the characteristic attitude of alarm, ears spread like dark flags. Somehow he portrayed the whole vastness and timelessness of a continent, and yet he was at bay, and one sensed that all his great strength was unavailing, that he was confused by things that were beyond his experience and the trace memories of his ancestors, that he was about to be overwhelmed by change—like Africa itself.

Shown, too, in the photograph was the land, the rich red earth riven by wind, baked by sun, ruined by drought. Craig could almost taste the dust on his tongue. Then, over it all, the limitless sky, containing the promise of succour, the silver cumulus nimbus piled like a snow-clad mountain range, bruised with purple and royal blue, pierced by a single beam of light from a hidden sun that fell on the old bull like a benediction.

She had captured the meaning and the mystery of his native land in the five hundredth of a second that it took the lens shutter to open and close again, while he had laboured for long agonizing months and not come anywhere near it, and, secretly recognizing his failure, was afraid to try again. He took a sip of the insipid wine that had been offered to him as a rebuke for this crisis of confidence, and now the wine had a quinine after-taste that he had not noticed before.

"Where are you from?" he asked the girl, without looking at her.

"Denver, Colorado," she said. "But my father has been with the Embassy in London for years. I did most of my schooling in England." That accounted for the accent. "I went to Africa when I was eighteen, and fell in love with it," she said, completing her life story simply.

It took a physical effort for Craig to touch the photograph and gently turn it face down. Beneath it was another of a young woman seated on a black lava rock beside a desert water-hole. She wore the distinctive leather bunny-ears headdress of the Ovahimba tribe. Her child stood beside her and nursed from her naked breast. The woman's skin was polished with fat and ochre. Her eyes were those from a fresco in a Pharaoh's tomb, and she was beautiful.

"Denver, Colorado, forsooth!" Craig thought and was surprised at his own bitterness, at the depths of his sudden resentment. How dare a damned foreign girl-child encapsulate so unerringly the complex spirit of a people in this portrait of a young woman. He had lived all his life with them and yet never seen an African so clearly as at this moment in an Italian restaurant in Greenwich Village.

He turned the photograph with a suppressed violence. Beneath it was a view into the trumpet-shaped throat of the magnificent maroon and gold bloom of *Kigelia africana,* Craig's favourite wild flower. In the lustrous depths of the flower nestled a tiny beetle like a precious emerald, shiny iridescent green. It was a perfect arrangement of shape and colour, and he found he hated her for it.

There were many others. One of a grinning lout of a militiaman with an AK 47 rifle on his shoulder and necklace of cured human ears around his neck, a caricature of savagery and arrogance; another of a wrinkled witch-doctor hung with horns and beads and skulls and all the grisly accoutrements of his trade, his patient stretched out on the bare, dusty earth before him in the process of being crudely cupped, her blood making shiny serpents across her skin. The patient was a woman in her prime with patterns of tattoos on her breasts and cheeks and forehead. Her teeth were filed to points like those of a shark, a relic of the days of cannibalism, and her eyes, like those of a suffering animal, seemed filled with all the stoicism and patience of Africa.

Then there was another contrasting photograph of African children in a schoolroom of poles and rude thatch. They shared a single book between three of them, but all their hands were raised eagerly to the young black teacher's questions and all their faces lit by the burning desire for knowledge—it was all there, a complete record of hope and despair, of abject poverty and great riches, of savagery and tenderness, of unrelenting elements and bursting fruitfulness, of pain and gentle humour. Craig could not bring himself to look at the photographer again and he turned the stiff glossy sheets slowly, savouring each image and delaying the moment when he must face her.

Craig stopped suddenly, struck by a particularly poignant composition, an orchard of bleached bones. She had used black and white to heighten the dramatic effect, and the bones shone in the brilliant African sunlight, acres of bones, great femur and tibia bleached like driftwood, huge rib cages like the frames of stranded ocean clippers, and skulls the size of beer barrels with darkened caves for eye sockets. Craig thought of the legendary elephants' graveyard, the old hunters' myth of the secret place where the elephants go to die.

"Poachers," she said. "Two hundred and eighty-six carcasses," and now Craig looked up at her at last, startled by the number.

"At one time?" he asked, and she nodded.

"They drove them into one of the old minefields."

Involuntarily, Craig shuddered and looked down at the photograph again. Under the table-top his right hand ran down his thigh until he felt the neat strap that held his leg, and he experienced a choking empathy for the fate of those great pachyderms. He remembered his own minefield, and felt again the slamming impact of the explosion into his foot, as though he had been hit by the full swing of a sledgehammer.

"I'm sorry," she said softly. "I know about your leg."

"She does her homework," Ashe said.

"Shut up," Craig thought furiously. "Why don't you both shut up." He hated anyone to mention the leg. If she had truly done her homework, she would have known that—but it was not only mention of the leg, it was the elephants also. Once Craig had worked as a ranger in the game department. He knew them, had come to love them, and the evidence of this slaughter sickened and appalled him. It increased his resentment of the girl; she had inflicted this upon him and he wanted to revenge himself, a childish urge to retaliate. But before he could do it, the late guest arrived, diverting them into a round of Ashe's introductions.

"Craig, I want you to meet a special sort of guy." All of Ashe's introductions came with a built-in commercial. "This is Henry Pickering. Henry is a senior vice-president of the World Bank—listen and you'll hear all those billions of dollars clashing around in his head. Henry, this is Craig Mellow, our boy genius. Not even excluding Karen Blixen, Craig is just one of the most important writers ever to come out of Africa, that's all he is!"

Henry nodded. "I read the book." He was very tall and thin and prematurely bald. He wore a grey banker's suit and stark white shirt, with a little individual touch of colour in his necktie and twinkly blue eyes. "For once you are probably not exaggerating, Ashe."

He kissed Sally-Anne's cheek platonically, sat down, tasted the wine that Ashe poured for him and pushed the glass back an inch. Craig found himself admiring his style.

"What do you think?" Henry Pickering asked Craig, glancing down at the open portfolio of photographs.

"He loves them, Henry," Ashe Levy cut in swiftly. "He's ape over them—I wish you could have seen his face when he got his first look—loves them, man, loves them!"

"Good," Henry said softly, watching Craig's face. "Have you explained the concept?"

Ashe Levy shook his head. "I wanted to serve it up hot. I wanted to hit him with it."

He turned to Craig.

"A book," he said. "It's about a book. The title of the book is 'Craig Mellow's Africa.' What happens is you write about the Africa of your ancestors, about what it was and what it has become. You go back and you do an in-depth assessment. You speak to the people—"

"Excuse me," Henry interrupted him, "I understand that you speak one of the two major languages—Sindebele, isn't it—of Zimbabwe?"

"Fluently," Ashe answered for Craig. "Like one of them."

Henry nodded. "Good. Is it true that you have many friends—some highly placed in government?"

Ashe fielded the question again. "Some of his old buddies are cabinet ministers in the Zimbabwe government. You can't go much higher."

Craig dropped his eyes to the photograph of the elephant graveyard. "Zimbabwe." He was not yet comfortable with the new name that the black victors had chosen. He still thought of it as Rhodesia. That was the country his ancestors had hacked out of the wilderness with pick and axe and Maxim machine-gun. Their land, once his land—by any name still his home.

"It's going to be top quality, Craig, no expense spared. You can go where you want to, speak to anybody, the World Bank will see to that, and pay for it." Ashe Levy was running on enthusiastically, and Craig looked up at Henry Pickering.

"The World Bank—publishing?" Craig asked sardonically, and when Ashe would have replied again, Henry Pickering laid a restraining hand on his forearm.

"I'll take the ball awhile, Ashe," he said. He had sensed Craig's mood; his tone was gentle and placatory. "The main part of our business is loans to underdeveloped countries. We have almost a billion invested in Zimbabwe. We want to protect our investment. Think of it as a prospectus; we want the world to know about the little African state that we would like to turn into a showpiece, an example of how a black government can succeed. We think your book could help do that for us."

"And these?" Craig touched the pile of photographs.

"We want the book to have visual as well as intellectual impact. We think Sally-Anne can provide that."

Craig was quiet for many seconds while he felt the terror slither around deep inside him, like some loathsome reptile. The terror of failure. Then he thought about having to compete with these photographs, of having to provide a text that would not be swamped by the awesome view through this girl's lens. He had a reputation at stake, and she had nothing to lose. The odds were all with her. She would be not an ally but an adversary, and his resentment came back in full force, so strong that it was a kind of hatred.

She was leaning towards him across the table, the spotlight catching her long eyelashes and framing those green-flecked eyes. Her mouth was quivering with eagerness, and a tiny bubble of saliva like a seed pearl sparkled on her lower lip. Even in his anger and fear, Craig wondered what it would be like to kiss that mouth.

"Craig," she said, "I can do better than those if I have the chance. I can go all the way, if you give me the chance. Please!"

"You like elephants?" Craig asked her. "I'll tell you an elephant story. The big old bull elephant had a flea that lived in his left ear. One day the elephant crossed a rickety bridge, and when he got to the other side, the flea said in his ear, 'Hoo boy! We sure rocked that bridge!' "

Sally-Anne's lips closed slowly and then paled. Her eyelids fluttered, the dark lashes beating like butterflies' wings, and as the tears began to sparkle behind them she leaned back out of the light.

There was a silence, and in it Craig felt a rush of remorse. He felt sickened by his own cruelty and pettiness. He had expected her to be tough and resilient, to come back with a barbed retort. He had not expected the tears. He wanted to comfort her, to tell her that he didn't mean it the way it sounded. He wanted to explain his own fear and insecurity, but she was rising and picking up the folio of photographs.

"Parts of your book were so understanding, so compassionate, I wanted so badly to work with you," she said softly. "I guess it was dumb to expect you to be like your book." She looked at Ashe. "I'm sorry, Ashe, I'm just not hungry any more."

Ashe Levy stood quickly. "We'll share a cab," he said. Then softly to Craig, "Well done, hero, call me when you've got the new typescript finished," and he hurried after Sally-Anne. As she went through the door the sunlight back-lit her and Craig saw the shape of her legs through her skirt. They were long and lovely, and then she was gone.

Henry Pickering was fiddling with his glass, studying the wine thoughtfully.

"It's pasteurized Roman goat urine," Craig said. He found his voice was uneven. He signalled the wine waiter and ordered a Meursault.

"That's better," Henry understated it. "Well, perhaps the book wasn't such a great idea after all, was it?" He glanced at his wrist-watch. "We'd better order."

They talked of other things—the Mexican loan default, Reagan's mid-term assessment, the gold price—Henry preferred silver for a quick appreciation and thought diamonds would soon be looking good again. "I'd buy De Beers to hold," he advised.

A svelte young blonde from one of the other tables came across while they were taking coffee.

"You're Craig Mellow," she accused him. "I saw you on TV. I loved your book. Please, please, sign this for me."

While he signed her menu, she leaned over him and pressed one hard hot little breast against his shoulder.

"I work at the cosmetics counter in Saks Fifth Ave," she breathed. "You can find me there any time." The odour of expensive, pilfered perfumes lingered after she had left.

"Do you always turn them away?" Henry asked a little wistfully.

Craig laughed. "Man is only flesh and blood."

Henry insisted on paying the tab. "I have a limo," he offered. "I could drop you."

"I'll walk off the pasta," Craig said.

"Do you know, Craig, I think you'll go back to Africa. I saw the way you looked at those photographs. Like a hungry man."

"It's possible."

"The book. Our interest in it. There was more to it than Ashe understood. You know the top blacks there. That interests me. The ideas you expressed in the book fit into our thinking. If you do decide to go back, call me before you do. You and I could do each other a favour."

Henry climbed into the back seat of the black Cadillac, and then with the door still open he said, "I thought her pictures were rather good, actually." He closed the door and nodded to the chauffeur.

*   *   *

Bawu was moored between two new commercially built yachts, a forty-five-foot Camper and Nicholson and a Hatteras convertible, and she stood the comparison well enough, although she was almost five years old. Craig had put in every screw with his own hands. He paused at the gates of the marina to look at her, but somehow today he did not derive as much pleasure as usual from her lines.

"Been a couple of calls for you, Craig," the girl behind the reception desk in the marina office called out to him and he went in. "You can use this phone."

He checked the slips she handed him, one from his broker marked "urgent," another from the literary editor of a midwestern daily. There hadn't been too many of those recently.

He phoned the broker first. They had sold the Mocatta gold certificates that he had bought for three hundred and twenty dollars an ounce at five hundred and two dollars. He instructed them to put the money on call deposit.

Then he dialled the second number. While he waited to be connected, the girl behind the desk moved around more than was really necessary, bending over the lowest drawers of the filing cabinet to give Craig a good look at what she had in her white Bermudas and pink halter-top.

When Craig connected with the literary editor, she wanted to know when they were publishing his new book.

"What book?" Craig thought bitterly, but he answered, "We haven't got a firm date yet—but it's in the pipeline. Do you want to do an interview in the meantime?"

"Thanks, but we will wait until publication, Mr. Mellow."

"Long wait, my darling," Craig thought, and when he hung up the girl looked up brightly.

"The party is on *Firewater* tonight." There was a party on one of the yachts every single night of the year. "Are you coming across?"

She had a flat tight belly between the shorts and top. Without the glasses, she might be quite pretty—and what the hell, he had just made a quarter of a million dollars on the gold certificates and a fool of himself at the lunch table.

"I'm having a private party on *Bawu*," he said, "for two." She had been a good patient girl and her time had come.

Her face lit up so he saw he had been right. She really was quite pretty. "I finish in here at five."

"I know," he said. "Come straight down."

Wipe one out and make another happy, he thought. It should even out, but of course it didn't.

*   *   *

Craig lay on his back under a single sheet in the wide bunk with both hands behind his head and listened to the small sounds in the night, the creak of the rudder in its restrainer, the tap of a halyard against the mast and the slap of wavelets under the hull. Across the basin the party on *Firewater* was still in full swing, there was a faint splash and a distant burst of drunken laughter as they threw somebody overboard, and beside him the girl made regular little wet fluttering sounds through her lips as she slept.

She had been eager and very practised, but nevertheless Craig felt unrequited and restless. He wanted to go up on deck, but that would have disturbed the girl and he knew she would still be eager and he could not be bothered further. So he lay and let the images from Sally-Anne's portfolio run through his head like a magic-lantern show, and they triggered others that had long lain dormant but now came back to him fresh and vivid, accompanied by the smells and tastes and sounds of Africa, so that instead of the revels of drunken yachties, he heard again the beat of native drums along the Chobe River in the night; instead of the sour waters of the East River he smelled tropical rain-drops on baked earth, and he began to ache with the bitter-sweet melancholy of nostalgia and he did not sleep again that night.

The girl insisted on making breakfast for him. She did so with not nearly the same expertise as she had made love, and after she had gone ashore it took him nearly an hour to clean up the galley. Then he went up to the saloon.

He drew the curtain across the porthole above his navigation and writing desk, so as not to be distracted by the activities of the marina, and settled down to work. He reread the last batch of ten pages, and realized he would be lucky if he could salvage two of them. He set to it grimly and the characters balked and said trite asinine things. After an hour he reached up for his thesaurus from the shelf beside his desk to find an alternative word.

"Good Lord, even I know that people don't say 'pusillanimous' in real conversation," he muttered as he brought down the volume, and then paused as a slim sheath of folded writing-paper fluttered out from between the pages.

Secretly welcoming the excuse to break off the struggle, he unfolded it, and with a little jolt discovered it was a letter from a girl called Janine—a girl who had shared with him the agonies of their war wounds, who had travelled with him the long slow road to recovery, had been at his side when he walked again for the first time after losing the leg, had spelled him at the helm when they sailed *Bawu* through her first Atlantic gale. A girl whom he had loved and almost married, and whose face he now had the greatest difficulty recalling.

Janine had written the letter from her home in Yorkshire, three days before she married the veterinary surgeon who was a junior partner in her father's practice. He reread the letter slowly, all ten pages of it, and realized why he had hidden it away from himself. Janine was only bitter in patches, but some of the other things she wrote cut deeply.

". . . You had been a failure so often and for so long that your sudden success clean bowled you . . ."

He checked at that. What else had he ever done besides the book— that one single book? And she had given him the answer.

". . . You were so innocent and gentle, Craig, so lovable in a gawky boyish way. I wanted to live with that, but after we left Africa it dried up slowly, you started becoming hard and cynical . . ."

". . . Do you remember the very first day we met, or almost the very first, I said to you, 'You are a spoilt little boy, and you just give up on everything worthwhile'? Well, it's true, Craig. You gave up on our relationship. I don't just mean the other little dolly-birds, the literary scalp-hunters with no elastic in their drawers, I mean you gave up on the caring. Let me give you a little advice for free, don't give up on the only thing that you've ever done well, don't give up on the writing, Craig. That would be truly sinful . . ."

He remembered how haughtily he had scoffed at that notion when he had first read it. He didn't scoff now—he was too afraid. It was happening to him, just as she had predicted.

"I truly came to love you, Craig, not all at once, but little by little. You had to work very hard to destroy that. I don't love you any more, Craig, I doubt I'll ever love another man, not even the one I'll marry on Saturday—but I like you, and I always will. I wish you well, but beware of your most implacable enemy—yourself."

Craig refolded the letter, and he wanted a drink. He went down to the galley and poured a Bacardi—a large one, easy on the lime. While he drank it he reread the letter and this time a single phrase struck him.

"After we left Africa it dried up slowly . . . the understanding, the genius."

"Yes," he whispered. "It dried up. It all dried up."

Suddenly his nostalgia became the unbearable ache of homesickness. He had lost his way, the fountain in him *had* dried up, and he wanted to go back to the source.

He tore the letter to tiny pieces and dropped them into the scummy waters of the basin, left the empty glass on the coaming of the hatch and crossed the gang-plank to the jetty.

He didn't want to have to talk to the girl, so he used the pay phone at the gate of the marina.

It was easier than he expected. The switchboard operator put him through to Henry Pickering's secretary.

"I'm not sure that Mr. Pickering is available. Who is calling, please?"

"Craig Mellow." Pickering came on almost immediately.

"There is an old Matabele saying, 'The man who drinks Zambezi waters must always return to drink again,' " Craig told him.

"So you're thirsty," Pickering said. "I guessed that."

"You said to call you."

"Come and see me."

"Today?" Craig asked.

"Hey, man, you're hot to trot! Hold on, let me check my calendar— what about six o'clock this evening? That's the soonest I can work it in."

Henry's office was on the twenty-sixth floor and the tall windows faced up the deep sheer crevasses of the avenues to the expansive green swathe of Central Park in the distance.

Henry poured Craig a whisky and soda and brought it to him at the window. They stood looking down into the guts of the city and drinking in silence, while the big red ball of the sun threw weird shadows through the purpling dusk.

"I think it's time to stop being cute, Henry," Craig said at last. "Tell me what you really want from me."

"Perhaps you're right," Henry agreed. "The book was a little bit of a cover-up. Not really fair—although, speaking personally, I'd like to have seen your words with her pictures—"

Craig made an impatient little gesture, and Henry went on.

"I am vice-president in charge of the Africa division."

Craig nodded. "I saw your title on the door."

"Despite what a lot of our critics say, we aren't a charitable institution, we are one of the bulwarks of capitalism. Africa is a continent of economically fragile states. With the obvious exceptions of South Africa and the oil producers farther north, they are mostly subsistence agricultural societies, with no industrial backbone and very few mineral resources."

Craig nodded again.

"Some of those who have recently achieved their independence from the old colonial system are still benefitting from the infrastructure built up by the white settlers, while most of the others—Zambia and Tanzania and Maputo, for instance—have had long enough to let it run down into a chaos of lethargy and ideological fantasy. They are going to be hard to save." Henry shook his head mournfully and looked even more like an undertaker stork. "But with others, like Zimbabwe, Kenya and Malawi, we have got a fighting chance. The system is still working, as yet the farms haven't been totally decimated and handed over to hordes of peasant squatters, the railroads work, there are some foreign exchange earnings from copper and chrome and tourism. We can keep them going, with a little luck."

"Why bother?" Craig asked. "I mean, you said you are not in the charity game, so why bother?"

"Because if we don't feed them, then sooner or later we are going to have to fight them, it's as simple as that. If they begin to starve, guess into whose big red paws they are going to fall."

"Yes. You're making sense." Craig sipped his whisky.

"Returning to earth for a moment," Henry went on, "the countries on our shortlist have one exploitable asset, nothing tangible like gold, but many times more valuable. They are attractive to tourists from the west. If we are ever going to see any interest on the billions that we have got tied up in them, then we are going to have to make good and sure that they stay attractive."

"How do you do that?"

"Let's take Kenya as an example," Henry suggested. "Sure, it's got sunshine and beaches, but then so have Greece and Sardinia, and they are a hell of a lot closer to Paris and Berlin. What the Mediterranean hasn't got is African wildlife, and that's what the tourists will fly those extra hours to see, and that's the collateral on our loan. Tourist dollars are keeping us in business."

Craig frowned. "Okay, but I don't see how I come in."

"Wait for it, we'll get there in time," Henry told him. "Let me lay it out a little first. It's like this—unfortunately, the very first thing that the newly independent black African sees when he looks around after the white man flies out is ivory and rhinoceros horn and meat on the hoof. One rhinoceros or bull elephant represents more wealth than he could earn in ten years of honest labour. For fifty years a white-run game department has protected all these marvellous riches, but now the whites have run to Australia or Johannesburg, an Arab sheikh will pay twenty-five thousand dollars for a dagger with a genuine rhinoceros-horn handle and the victorious guerrilla fighter has an AK 47 rifle in his hands. It's all very logical."

Craig nodded. "Yes, I've seen it."

"We had the same thing in Kenya. Poaching was big business and it was run from the top. I mean the very top. It took us fifteen years and the death of a president to break it up. Now Kenya has the strictest game laws in Africa—and, more important, they are being enforced. We had to use all our influence. We even had to threaten to pull the plug, but now our investment is protected." Henry looked smug for a moment, then his melancholia overwhelmed him again. "Now we have to travel exactly the same road again in Zimbabwe. You saw those photographs of the kill in the minefield. It's being organized again, and once again we suspect it's somebody in a very high place. We have to stop it."

"I'm still waiting to hear how it affects me."

"I need an agent in the field. Somebody with experience—perhaps even somebody who once worked in the game and wildlife department, somebody who speaks the local language, who has a legitimate excuse for moving around and asking questions—perhaps an author researching a new book, who has contacts high up in government. Of course, if my agent has an international reputation, it would open even more doors, and if he were a dedicated proponent of the capitalist system and truly believed in what we are doing, he would be totally effective."

"James Bond, me?"

"Field investigator for the World Bank. The pay is forty thousand dollars a year, plus expenses and a lot of job satisfaction, and if there isn't a book in it at the end, I'll stand you to lunch at La Grenouille with the wine of your choice."

"Like I said at the beginning, Henry, isn't it time to stop being cute and level with me completely?"

It was the first time Craig had heard Henry laugh, and it was infectious, a warm, throaty chuckle.

"Your perception confirms the wisdom of my choice. All right, Craig, there is a little more to it. I didn't want to make it too complicated— not until you had got your feet wet first. Let me freshen your drink."

He went to the cocktail cabinet in the shape of an antique globe of the world, and while he clinked ice on glass he went on.

"It is vitally important for us to have a complete picture of what's going on below the surface in all of the countries in which we have an involvement. In other words, a functioning intelligence system. Our set-up in Zimbabwe isn't nearly as effective as I'd like it to be. We have lost a key man lately—motor car accident—or that's what it looked like. Before he went, he gave us a hint—he had picked up the rumours of a *coup d'état* backed by the Ruskies."

Craig sighed. "We Africans don't really put much store in the ballot box any more. The only things that count are tribal loyalties and a strong arm. *Coup d'état* makes better sense than votes."

"Are you on the team?" Henry wanted to know.

"I take it that 'expenses' include first-class air tickets?" Craig demanded wickedly.

"Every man has his price," Henry darted back, "is that yours?"

Craig shook his head. "I don't come that cheap, but I'd hate like hell to have a Soviet stooge running the land where my leg is buried. I'll take the job."

"Thought you might." Henry offered his hand. It was cool and startlingly powerful. "I'll send a messenger down to your yacht with a file and a survival kit. Read the file while the messenger waits and send it back. Keep the kit."

Henry Pickering's survival kit contained an assortment of press cards, a membership of the TWA Ambassadors Club, an unlimited World Bank Visa credit card, and an ornate metal and enamel star in a leather case embossed "Field Assessor—World Bank."

Craig weighed it in his palm. "You could beat a man-eating lion to death with it," he muttered. "I don't know what else it will be good for."

The file was a great deal more rewarding. When he finished reading it, he realized that the alteration of name from Rhodesia to Zimbabwe was probably one of the least drastic changes that had swept over the land of his birth since he had left it just a few short years before.

* * *

Craig nursed the hired Volkswagen over the undulating golden grass-clad hills, using an educated foot on the throttle. The Matabele girl at the Avis desk in the Bulawayo airport had cautioned him.

"The tank is full, sir, but I don't know when you will get another tankful. There is very little gasoline in Matabeleland."

In the town itself he had seen the vehicles parked in long lines at the filling stations, and the proprietor of the motel had briefed Craig as he signed the register and picked up the keys to one of the bungalows.

"The Maputo rebels keep hitting the pipeline from the east coast. The hell of it is that just across the border the South Africans have got it all and they are happy to deal, but our bright laddies don't want politically tainted gas, so the whole country grinds to a halt. A plague on political dreams—to exist we have to deal with all kinds of people and it's about time they accepted that."

So now Craig drove with care, and the gentle pace suited him. It gave him time to examine the familiar countryside, and to assess the changes that the years had wrought.

He turned off the main macadamized road fifteen miles out of town, and took the yellow dirt road to the north. Within a mile he reached the boundary, and saw immediately that the gate hung at a drunken angle and was wide open—the first time he had ever seen it that way. He parked and tried to close it behind him, but the frame was buckled and the hinges had rusted. He abandoned the effort and left the road to examine the sign that lay in the grass.

The sign had been pulled down, the retaining bolts ripped clear out. It lay face up, and, though sun-faded, was still legible:

KING'S LYNN AFRIKANDER STUD
HOME OF "BALLANTYNE'S ILLUSTRIOUS IV"
GRAND CHAMPION OF CHAMPIONS
PROPRIETOR: JONATHAN BALLANTYNE

Craig had a vivid mental image of the huge red beast with its humped back and swinging dewlap waddling under its own weight of beef around the show-ring with the blue rosette of the champion on its cheek, and Jonathan "Bawu" Ballantyne, Craig's maternal grandfather, leading it proudly by the brass ring through its shiny wet nostrils.

Craig walked back to the VW and drove on through grassland that had once been thick and gold and sweet, but through which the bare dusty earth now showed like the balding scalp of a middle-aged man. He was distressed by the condition of the grazing. Never, not even in the four-year drought of the fifties, had King's Lynn grass been allowed to deteriorate like this, and Craig could find no reason for it until he stopped again beside a clump of camel-thorn trees that threw their shade over the road.

When he switched off the engine, he heard the bleating among the camel thorns and now he was truly shocked.

"Goats!" he spoke aloud. "They are running goats on King's Lynn." Bawu Ballantyne's ghost must be without rest or peace. Goats on his beloved grassland. Craig went to look for them. There were two hundred or more in one herd. Some of the agile multicoloured animals had climbed high into the trees and were eating bark and seedpods, while others were cropping the grass down to the roots so that it would die and the soil would sour. Craig had seen the devastation that these animals had created in the tribal trustlands.

There were two naked Matabele boys with the herd. They were delighted when Craig spoke to them in their own language. They stuffed the cheap candy that he had brought with him for just such a meeting into their cheeks, and chattered without inhibition.

Yes, there were thirty families living on King's Lynn now, and each family had its herd—the finest goats in Matabeleland, they boasted through sticky lips, and under the trees a horned old billy mounted a young nanny with a vigorous humping of his neck. "See!" cried the herdboys, "they breed with a will. Soon we will have more goats than any of the other families."

"What happened to the white farmers that lived here?" Craig asked.

"Gone!" they told him proudly. "Our warriors drove them back to where they came from and now the land belongs to the children of the revolution."

They were six years old, but still they had the revolutionary cant word-perfect.

Each of the children had a slingshot made from old rubber tubing hanging from his neck, and around his naked waist a string of birds that he had killed with the slingshot: larks and warblers and jewelled sunbirds. Craig knew that for their noon meal they would cook them whole on a bed of coals, simply letting the feathers sizzle off and devouring the tiny blackened carcasses with relish. Old Bawu Ballantyne would have strapped any herdboy that he caught with a slingshot.

The herdboys followed Craig back to the road, begged another piece of candy from him and waved him away like an old dear friend. Despite the goats and songbirds, Craig felt again the overwhelming affection for these people. They were, after all, his people and it was good to be home again.

He stopped again on the crest of the hills and looked down on the homestead of King's Lynn. The lawns had died from lack of attention, and the goats had been in the flower-beds. Even at this distance, Craig could see that the main house was deserted. Windows were broken, leaving unsightly gaps like missing teeth, and most of the asbestos sheets had been stolen from the roof and the roof-timbers were forlorn and skeletal against the sky. The roofing sheets had been used to build ramshackle squatters' shacks down near the old cattle-pens.

Craig drove down and parked beside the dip tank. The tank was dry, and half-filled with dirt and rubbish. He went past it to the squatters' encampment. There were half a dozen families living here. Craig scattered the yapping cur dogs that rushed out at him with a few well-aimed stones, then greeted the old man who sat at one of the fires.

"I see you, old father." Again there was delight at his command of the language. He sat at the fire for an hour, chatting with the old Matabele, the words coming more and more readily to his tongue and his ear tuning to the rhythm and nuances of Sindebele. He learned more than he had in the four days since he had been back in Matabeleland.

"They told us that after the revolution every man would have a fine motor car, and five hundred head of the best white man's cattle." The old man spat into the fire. "The only ones with motor cars are the government ministers. They told us we would always have full bellies, but food costs five times what it did before Smith and the white men ran away. Everything costs five times more—sugar and salt and soap—everything."

During the white regime a ferocious foreign exchange control system and a rigid internal price control structure had isolated the country from the worst effects of inflation, but now they were experiencing all the joys of re-entering the international community, and the local currency had already been devalued twenty per cent.

"We cannot afford cattle," the old man explained, "so we run goats.

Goats!" He spat again into the fire and watched his phlegm sizzle. "Goats! Like dirt-eating Shona." His tribal hatred boiled like his spittle.

Craig left him muttering and frowning over the smoky fire and walked up to the house. As he climbed the steps to the wide front veranda, he had a weird premonition that his grandfather would suddenly come out to meet him with some tart remark. In his mind's eye he saw again the old man, dapper and straight, with thick silver hair, skin like tanned leather and impossibly green Ballantyne eyes, standing before him.

"Home again, Craig, dragging your tail behind you!"

However, the veranda was littered with rubble and bird-droppings from the wild pigeons that roosted undisturbed in the rafters.

He picked his way along the veranda to the double doors that led into the old library. There had been two huge elephant tusks framing this doorway, the bull which Craig's great-great-grandfather had shot back in the 1860s. Those tusks were family heirlooms, and had always guarded the entrance to King's Lynn. Old grandpa Bawu had touched them each time he passed, so that there had been a polished spot on the yellow ivory. Now there were only the holes in the masonry from which the bolts holding the ivory had been torn. The only family relics he had inherited and still owned were the collection of leatherbound family journals, the laboriously hand-written records of his ancestors from the arrival of his great-great-grandfather in Africa over a hundred years before. The tusks would complement the old books. He would search for them, he promised himself. Surely such rare treasures must be traceable.

He went into the derelict house. The shelving and built-in cupboards and floor-boards had been stripped out by the squatters in the valley for firewood, the window-panes used as targets by small black boys with slingshots. The books, the portrait photographs from the walls, the carpets and heavy furniture of Rhodesian teak were all gone. The homestead was a shell, but a sturdy shell. With an open palm Craig slapped the walls that great-great-grandfather Zouga Ballantyne had built of hand-hewn stone and mortar that had had almost a hundred years to cure to adamantine hardness. His palm made a solid ringing tone. It would take only a little imagination and a great deal of money to transform the shell into a magnificent home once again.

Craig left the house and climbed the kopje behind it to the walled family cemetery that lay under the msasa trees beneath the rocky crest. There was grass growing up between the headstones. The cemetery had been neglected but not vandalized, as had many of the other monuments left from the colonial era.

Craig sat on the edge of his grandfather's grave and said, "Hello, Bawu. I'm back," and started as he almost heard the old man's voice, full of mock scorn speaking in his mind.

"Yes, every time you burn your arse you come running back here. What happened this time?"

"I dried up, Bawu," he answered the accusation aloud and then was silent. He sat for a long time and very slowly he felt the tumult within him begin to subside.

"The place is in a hell of a mess, Bawu," he spoke again, and the little blue-headed lizard on the old man's headstone scuttled away at the sound of his voice. "The tusks are gone from the veranda, and they are running goats on your best grass."

Again he was silent, but now he was beginning to calculate and scheme. He sat for nearly an hour, and then stood up.

"Bawu, how would you like it if I could move the goats off your pasture?" he asked, and walked back down the hill to where he had left the Volkswagen.

*   *   *

It was a little before five o'clock when he drove back into town. The estate agency and auctioneering floor opposite the Standard Bank was still open for business. The sign had even been repainted in scarlet, and as soon as Craig entered, he recognized the burly red-faced auctioneer in khaki shorts and short-sleeved, open-necked shirt.

"So you didn't take the gap, like the rest of us did, Jock," Craig said, greeting Jock Daniels.

"Taking the gap" was the derogatory expression for emigrating. Out of 250,000 white Rhodesians, almost 150,000 had taken the gap since the beginning of hostilities, and most of those had left since the war had been lost and the black government of Robert Mugabe had taken control.

Jock stared at him. "Craig!" he exploded. "Craig Mellow!" He took Craig's hand in a horny brown paw. "No, I stayed, but sometimes it gets hellish lonely. But you've done well, by God you have. They say in the papers that you have made a million out of that book. People here could hardly believe it. Old Craig Mellow, they said, fancy Craig Mellow of all people."

"Is that what they said?" Craig's smile stiffened, and he took his hand back.

"Can't say I liked the book myself." Jock shook his head. "You made all the blacks look like bloody heroes—but that's what they like overseas, isn't it? Black is beautiful—that's what sells books, hey?"

"Some of my reviewers called me a racist," Craig murmured. "You can't keep all the people happy all of the time."

Jock wasn't listening. "Another thing, Craig, why did you have to make out that Mr. Rhodes was a queer?"

Cecil Rhodes, the father of the white settlers, had been dead for eighty years, but the old-timers still called him Mr. Rhodes.

"I gave the reasons in the book." Craig tried to placate him.

"He was a great man, Craig, but nowadays it's the fashion for you young people to tear down greatness—like mongrels snapping at the heels of a lion." Craig could see that Jock was warming to his subject, and he had to divert him.

"How about a drink, Jock?" he asked, and Jock paused. His rosy cheeks and swollen purple nose were not solely the products of the African sun.

"Now, you're making sense." Jock licked his lips. "It's been a long thirsty day. Just let me lock up the shop."

"If I fetched a bottle, we could drink it here and talk privately."

The last of Jock's antagonism evaporated. "Damn good idea. The bottle store has a few bottles of Dimple Haig left—and get a bucket of ice while you are about it."

They sat in Jock's tiny cubicle of an office and drank the good whisky out of cheap thick tumblers. Jock's mood mellowed perceptively.

"I didn't leave, Craig, because there was nowhere to go. England? I haven't been back there since the war. Trade unions and bloody weather—no thanks. South Africa? They are going to go the same way that we did—at least we've got it over and done with." He poured again from the pinch bottle. "If you do go, they let you take two hundred dollars with you. Two hundred dollars to start again when you are sixty-five years old—no bloody thanks."

"So what's life like, Jock?"

"You know what they call an optimist here?" Jock asked. "It's somebody who believes that things can't get any worse." He bellowed with laughter and slapped his bare hairy thigh. "No. I'm kidding. It's not too bad. As long as you don't expect the old standards, if you keep your mouth shut and stay away from politics, you can still live a good life—probably as good as anywhere in the world."

"The big farmers and ranchers—how are they doing?"

"They are the elite. The government has come to its senses. They've dropped all that crap about nationalizing the land. They've come to face the fact that if they are going to feed the black masses, then they need the white farmers. They are becoming quite proud of them: when they get a state visitor—a communist Chinese or a Libyan minister—they give him a tour of white farms to show him how good things are looking."

"What about the price of land?"

"At the end of the war, when the blacks first took over and were shouting about taking the farms and handing them over to the masses, you couldn't give the land away." Jock gargled with his whisky. "Take your family company for instance, Rholands Ranching Company—that includes all three spreads: King's Lynn, Queen's Lynn and that big piece of country up in the north bordering the Chizarira Game Reserve —your uncle Douglas sold the whole damned shooting match for quarter of a million dollars. Before the war he could have asked ten million."

"Quarter of a million." Craig was shocked. "He gave it away!"

"That included all the stock—prize Afrikander bulls and breeding cows, the lot," Jock related with relish. "You see, he had to get out. He had been a member of Smith's cabinet from the beginning and he knew that he was a marked man once the black government took over. He sold out to a Swiss-German consortium, and they paid him in Zürich. Old Dougie took his family and went to Aussie. Of course, he already had a few million outside the country, so he could buy himself a nice little cattle station up in Queensland. It's us poor buggers with everything we have tied up here that had to stay."

"Have another drink," Craig offered, and then steered Jock back to Rholands Ranching. "What did the consortium do with Rholands?"

"Cunning bloody Krauts!" Jock was slurring a little by now. "They took all the stock, bribed somebody in government to give them an export permit, and shipped them over the border to South Africa. I hear they sold for almost a million and a half down there. Remember, they were the very top breeding-stock, champions of champions. So they cleared over a million, and then they repatriated their profit in gold shares and made another couple of million."

"They stripped the ranches and now they have abandoned them?" Craig asked, and Jock nodded weightily.

"They're trying to sell the company, of course. I've got it on my books—but it would take a pile of capital to restock the ranches and get them going again. Nobody is interested. Who wants to bring money into a country which is tottering on the brink? Answer me that!"

"What is the asking price for the company?" Craig inquired airily, and Jock Daniels sobered miraculously, and fastened Craig with a beady auctioneer's eye.

"You wouldn't be interested?" And his eye became beadier. "Did you really make a million dollars out of that book?"

"What are they asking?" Craig repeated.

"Two million. That's why I haven't found a buyer. Lots of the local boys would love to get their paws on that grazing—but two million. Who the hell has that kind of money in this country—"

"Supposing they could be paid in Zürich, would that make a difference to the price?" Craig asked.

"Do a Shona's armpits stink!"

"How much difference?"

"They might take a million—in Zürich."

"A quarter of a million?"

"No ways, never—not in ten thousand years," Jock shook his head emphatically.

"Telephone them. Tell them the ranches are overrun with squatters, and it would cause a political hoo-ha to try and move them now. Tell them they are running goats on the grazing, and in a year's time it will be a desert. Point out they will be getting their original investment out intact. Tell them the government has threatened to seize all land owned by absentee landlords. They could lose the lot."

"All that is true," Jock grumped. "But a quarter of a million! You are wasting my time."

"Phone them."

"Who pays for the call?"

"I do. You can't lose, Jock."

Jock sighed with resignation. "All right, I'll call."

"When?"

"Friday today—no point in calling until Monday."

"All right, in the meantime can you get me a few cans of gas?" Craig asked.

"What do you want gas for?"

"I'm going up to the Chizarira. I haven't been up there for ten years. If I'm going to buy it, I'd like to look at it again."

"I wouldn't do that, Craig. That's bandit country."

"The polite term is political dissidents."

"They are Matabele bandits," Jock said heavily, "and they'll either shoot your arse full of more holes than you can use, or they will kidnap you for ransom—or both."

"You get me some gas and I'll take the chance. I'll be back early next week to hear what your pals in Zürich have to say about the offer."

*   *   *

It was marvellous country, still wild and untouched—no fences, no cultivated lands, no buildings—protected from the influx of cattle and peasant farmers by the tsetse-fly belt which ran up from the Zambezi valley into the forests along the escarpment.

On the one side it was bounded by the Chizarira Game Reserve and on the other by the Mzolo Forest Reserve, both of which areas were vast reservoirs of wildlife. During the depression of the 1930s, old Bawu had chosen the country with care and paid sixpence an acre for it. One hundred thousand acres for two thousand five hundred pounds. "Of course, it will never be cattle country," he told Craig once, as they camped under the wild fig trees beside a deep green pool of the Chizarira River and watched the sand-grouse come slanting down on quick wings across the setting sun to land on the sugar-white sandbank beneath the far shore. "The grazing is sour, and the tsetse will kill anything you try to rear here—but for that reason it will always be an unspoiled piece of old Africa."

The old man had used it as a shooting lodge and a retreat. He had never strung barbed-wire or built even a shack on the ground, preferring to sleep on the bare earth under the spreading branches of the wild fig.

Very selectively Bawu had hunted here—elephant and lion and rhinoceros and buffalo—only the dangerous game, but he had jealously protected them from other rifles. Even his own sons and grandsons had been denied hunting rights.

"It's my own little private paradise," he told Craig, "and I'm selfish enough to keep it like that."

Craig doubted that the track through to the pools had been used since he and the old man had last been here together ten years before. It was totally overgrown, elephant had pushed mopani trees down like primitive road-blocks, and heavy rains had washed it out.

"Eat your heart out, Mr. Avis," said Craig, and put the sturdy little Volkswagen to it.

However, the front-wheel-drive vehicle was light enough and nippy enough to negotiate even the most unfriendly dry river-beds, although Craig had to corduroy the bottoms with branches to give it purchase in the fine sand. He lost the track half a dozen times, and only found it after laboriously casting ahead on foot.

He hit one ant-bear hole and had to jack up the front end to get out, and half the time he was finding ways round the elephant road-blocks. In the end he had to leave the Volkswagen and cover the last few miles on foot. He reached the pools in the final glimmering of daylight.

He curled up in the single blanket that he had filched from the motel, and slept through without dreaming or stirring, to wake in the ruddy magic of an African dawn. He ate cold baked beans out of the can and brewed coffee, then he left his pack and blanket under the wild figs and went down along the bank of the river.

On foot he could cover only a tiny portion of the wide wedge of wild country that spread over a hundred thousand acres, but the Chizarira River was the heart and artery of it. What he found here would allow him to judge what changes there had been since his last visit.

Almost immediately he realized that there were still plenty of the more common varieties of wildlife in the forest: the big, spooky, spiral-horned kudu went bounding away, flicking their fluffy white tails, and graceful little impala drifted like roseate smoke among the trees. Then he found signs of the rarer animals. First, the fresh pug-marks of a leopard in the clay at the water's edge where the cat had drunk during the night, and then, the elongated teardrop-shaped spoor and grapelike droppings of the magnificent sable antelope.

For his lunch he ate slices of dried sausage which he cut with his clasp-knife and sucked lumps of tart white cream of tartar from the pods of the baobab tree. When he moved on he came to an extensive stand of dense wild ebony bush, and followed one of the narrow twisting game trails into it. He had gone only a hundred paces when he came on a small clearing in the midst of the thicket of interwoven branches, and he experienced a surge of elation.

The clearing stank like a cattle-pen, but even ranker and gamier. He recognized it as an animal midden, a dunghill to which an animal returns habitually to defecate. From the character of the faeces, composed of digested twigs and bark, and from the fact that these had been churned and scattered, Craig knew immediately that it was a midden of the black rhinoceros, one of Africa's rarest and most endangered species.

Unlike its cousin the white rhinoceros, who is a grazer on grassland and a lethargic and placid animal, the black rhinoceros is a browser on the lower branches of the thick bush which it frequents. By nature it is a cantankerous, inquisitive, stupid and nervously irritable animal. It will charge anything that annoys it, including men, horses, trucks and even locomotives.

Before the war, one notorious beast had lived on the escarpment of the Zambezi valley where both road and railway began the plunge down towards the Victoria Falls. It had piled up a score of eighteen trucks and buses, catching them on a steep section of road where they were reduced to a walking pace, and taking them head-on so that its horn crunched through the radiator in a burst of steam. Then, perfectly satisfied, it would trot back into the thick bush with squeals of triumph.

Puffed up with success, it finally overreached itself when it took on the Victoria Falls express, lumbering down the tracks like a medieval knight in the jousting lists. The locomotive was doing twenty miles per hour and the rhinoceros weighed two tons and was making about the same speed in the opposite direction, so the meeting was monumental. The express came to a grinding halt with wheels spinning helplessly, but the rhinoceros had reached the end of his career as a wrecker of radiators.

The latest deposit of dung on the midden had been within the preceding twelve hours, Craig estimated with delight, and the spoor indicated a family group of bull and cow with calf at heel. Smiling, Craig recalled the old Matabele myth which accounted for the rhino's habit of scattering its dung, and for its fear of the porcupine—the only animal in all the bush from which it would fly in snorting panic.

The Matabele related that once upon a time a rhino had borrowed a quill from the porcupine to sew up a tear caused by a thorn in his thick hide. The rhino promised to return the quill at their next meeting. After repairing the rent with bark twine, the rhino placed the quill between his lips while he admired his handiwork, and inadvertently swallowed it. Now he is still searching for the quill, and assiduously avoiding the porcupine's recriminations.

The total world-wide population of the black rhinoceros probably did not exceed a few thousand and to have them still surviving here delighted Craig and made his tentative plans for the area much more viable.

Still grinning, he followed the freshest tracks away from the midden, hoping for a sighting, and had gone only half a mile when, just beyond the wall of impenetrable bush that flanked the narrow trail, there was a sudden hissing, churring outcry of alarm calls and a cloud of brown ox-peckers rose above the scrub. These noisy birds lived in a symbiotic relationship with the larger African game animals, feeding exclusively on the ticks and bloodsucking flies that infested them, and in return acting as wary sentinels to warn of danger.

Swiftly following the alarm, there was a deafening chuffing and snorting like that of a steam engine: with a crash, the bush parted and Craig got his longed-for sighting as an enormous grey beast burst out onto the path not thirty paces ahead of him and, still uttering blasts of affronted indignation, peered short-sightedly over its long polished double horns for something to charge.

Aware that the beast's weak eyes could not distinguish a motionless man at more than fifteen paces, and that the light breeze was blowing directly into his face, Craig stood frozen but poised to hurl himself to one side if the charge came his way. The rhino was switching his bulk from side to side with startling agility, the din of his ire unabated, and in Craig's fevered imagination his horn seemed to grow longer and sharper every second. Stealthily he reached for the clasp-knife in his pocket. The beast sensed the movement and trotted a half dozen paces closer, so that Craig was on the periphery of his effective vision and in serious danger at last.

Using a short underhanded flick, he tossed the knife high over the beast's head into the ebony thicket behind it, and there was a loud clatter as it struck a branch.

Instantly the rhino spun around and launched its huge body in a full and furious charge at the sound. The bush opened as though before a centurion tank, and the clattering, crashing charge dwindled swiftly as the rhinoceros kept going up the side of the hill and over the crest in search of an adversary. Craig sat down heavily in the middle of the path and doubled over with breathless laughter in which were echoes of mild hysteria.

Within the next few hours, Craig had found three of the pans of stinking, stagnant water that these strange beasts prefer to the clean running water of the river, and he had decided where to site the hides from which his tourists could view them at close range. Of course, he would furnish salt-licks beside the water-holes to make them even more attractive to the beasts, and bring them in to be photographed and gawked at.

Sitting on a log, beside one of the water-holes, he reviewed the factors that favoured his plans. It was under an hour's flight from here to the Victoria Falls, one of the seven natural wonders of the world, that already attracted thousands of tourists each month. It would be only a short detour to his camp here, so that added little to the tourists' original airfare. He had an animal that very few other reserves or camps could offer, together with most of the other varieties of game, concentrated in a relatively small area. He had undeveloped reservations on both boundaries to ensure a permanent source of interesting animal life.

What he had in mind was a champagne and caviar type of camp, on the lines of those private estates bordering the Kruger National Park in South Africa. He would put up small camps, sufficiently isolated from each other so as to give the occupants the illusion of having the wilderness to themselves. He would provide charismatic and knowledgeable guides to take his tourists by Land-Rover and on foot close to rare and potentially dangerous animals and make an adventure of it, and luxurious surroundings when they returned to camp in the evening—airconditioning and fine food and wines, pretty young hostesses to pamper them, wildlife movies and lectures by experts to instruct and entertain them. And he would charge them outrageously for it all, aiming at the very upper level of the tourist trade.

It was after sunset when Craig limped back into his rudimentary camp under the wild figs, his face and arms reddened by the sun, tsetsefly bites itching and swollen on the back of his neck, and the stump of his leg tender and aching from the unaccustomed exertions. He was too tired to eat. He unstrapped his leg, drank a single whisky from the plastic mug, rolled into his blanket and was almost immediately asleep. He woke for a few minutes during the night, and while he urinated he listened with sleepy pleasure to the distant roaring of a pride of hunting lions, and then returned to his blanket.

He was awakened by the whistling cries of the green pigeons feasting on the wild figs above his head, and found he was ravenously hungry and happy as he could not remember being for years.

After he had eaten, he hopped down to the water's edge, carrying a rolled copy of the *Farmers' Weekly* magazine, the African farmers' bible. Then, seated in the shallows with the coarse-sugar sand pleasantly rough under his naked backside and the cool green waters soothing his still aching stump, he studied the prices of stock offered for sale in the magazine and did mental arithmetic.

His ambitious plans were swiftly moderated when he realized what it would cost to restock King's Lynn and Queen's Lynn with thorough-bred bloodstock. The consortium had sold the original stud for a million and a half, and prices had gone up since then.

He would have to begin with good bulls, and grade cows—slowly build up his blood-lines. Still, that would cost plenty, the ranches would have to be re-equipped, and the development of the tourist camp here on the Chizarira River was going to cost another bundle. Then he would have to move the squatter families and their goats off his grazing —the only way to do that was to offer them financial compensation. Old grandfather Bawu had always told him, "Work out what you think it will cost, then double it. That way you will come close."

Craig threw the magazine up onto the bank and lay back with only his head above water while he did his sums.

On the credit side, he had lived frugally aboard the yacht, unlike a lot of other suddenly successful authors. The book had been on the best-seller lists on both sides of the Atlantic for almost a year, main choice of three major book clubs, Reader's Digest Condensed books, the TV series, paperback contracts, translations into a number of foreign languages, including Hindi—even though, at the end, the taxman had got in among his earnings.

Then again he had been lucky with what was left to him after these depredations. He had speculated in gold and silver, had made three good coups on the stock exchange, and finally had transferred most of his winnings into Swiss francs at the right time. Added to that, he could sell the yacht. A month earlier he had been offered a hundred and fifty thousand dollars for *Bawu*, but he would hate to part with it. Apart from that, he could try hitting Ashe Levy for a substantial advance on the undelivered novel and hock his soul in the process.

He reached the bottom line of his calculations and decided that if he pulled out all the stops, and used up all his lines of credit, he might be able to raise a million and a half, which would leave him short by at least as much again.

"Henry Pickering, my very favourite banker, are you ever in for a surprise!" He grinned recklessly as he thought of how he was planning to break the first and cardinal rule of the prudent investor and put it all in one basket. "Dear Henry, you have been selected by our computer to be the lucky lender of one and a half big Ms to a one-legged dried-up sometime scribbler." That was the best he could come up with at the moment, and it wasn't really worth worrying seriously until he had an answer from Jock Daniels' consortium. He switched to more mundane considerations.

He ducked down and sucked a mouthful of the sweet clear water. The Chizarira was a lesser tributary of the great Zambezi, so he was drinking Zambezi waters again, as he had told Henry Pickering he must. "Chizarira" was a hell of a mouthful for a tourist to pronounce, let alone remember. He needed a name under which to sell his little African paradise.

"Zambezi Waters," he said aloud. "I'll call it Zambezi Waters," and then almost choked as very close to where he lay a voice said clearly, "He must be a mad man."

It was a deep melodious Matabele voice. "First, he comes here alone and unarmed, and then he sits among the crocodiles and talks to the trees!"

Craig rolled over swiftly onto his belly, and stared at the three men who had come silently out of the forest and now stood on the bank, ten paces away, watching him with closed, expressionless faces.

They were, all three of them, dressed in faded denims—the uniform of the bush fighters—and the weapons they carried with casual familiarity were the ubiquitous AK 47s with the distinctive curved black magazine and laminated woodwork.

Denim, AK 47s and Matabele—no doubt in Craig's mind who these were. Regular Zimbabwean troops now wore jungle fatigues or battle-jackets, most were armed with Nato weapons and spoke the Shona language. These were former members of the disbanded Zimbabwe People's Revolutionary Army, now turned political rebels, men subject to no laws, nor higher authority, forged by a long murderous and bloody bush war into hard, ruthless men with death in their hands and death in their eyes. Although Craig had been warned of the possibility, and had indeed been half-expecting this meeting, still the shock made him feel dry-mouthed and nauseated.

"We don't have to take him," said the youngest of the three guerrillas. "We can shoot him and bury him secretly—that is good as a hostage." He was under twenty-five years of age, Craig guessed, and had probably killed a man for every year of his life.

"The six hostages we took on the Victoria Falls road gave us weeks of trouble, and in the end we had to shoot them anyway," agreed the second guerrilla, and they both looked to the third man. He was only a few years older than they were, but there was no doubt that he was the leader. A thin scar ran from the corner of his mouth up his cheek into the hairline at the temple. It puckered his mouth into a lopsided, sardonic grin.

Now Craig remembered the incident that they were discussing. Guerrillas had stopped a tourist bus on the main Victoria Falls road and abducted six men, Canadian, Americans and a Briton, and taken them into the bush as hostages for the release of political detainees. Despite an intensive search by police and regular army units, none of the hostages had been recovered.

The scarred leader stared at Craig with smoky dark eyes for long seconds, and then, with his thumb, slid the rate-of-fire selector on his rifle to automatic.

"A true Matabele does not kill a blood brother of the tribe." It took Craig an enormous effort to keep his voice steady, devoid of any trace of terror. His Sindebele was so flawless and easy that it was the leader of the guerrillas who blinked.

"Hau!" he said, which is an expression of amazement. "You speak like a man—but who is this blood brother you boast of?"

"Comrade Minister Tungata Zebiwe," Craig answered, and saw the instant shift in the man's gaze, and the sudden discomfiture of his two companions. He had hit a chord that had unbalanced them, and had delayed his own execution for the moment, but the leader's rifle was still cocked and on fully automatic, still pointed at his belly.

It was the youngster who broke the silence, speaking too loudly, to cover his own uncertainty. "It is easy for a baboon to shout the name of the black-maned lion from the hilltop, and claim his protection, but does the lion recognize the baboon? Kill him, I say, and have done with it."

"Yet he speaks like a brother," murmured the leader, "and Comrade Tungata is a hard man—"

Craig realized that his life was still at desperate risk. A little push either way was all that was needed.

"I will show you," he said, still without the slightest quaver in his voice. "Let me go to my pack."

The leader hesitated.

"I am naked," Craig told him. "No weapons—not even a knife—and you are three, with guns."

"Go!" the Matabele agreed. "But go with care. I have not killed a man for many moons—and I feel the lack."

Craig stood up carefully from the water and saw the interest in their eyes as they studied his leg foreshortened halfway between knee and ankle, and the compensating muscular development of the other leg and the rest of his body. The interest changed to wary respect as they saw how quickly and easily Craig moved on one leg. He reached his pack with water running down the hard flat muscles of chest and belly. He had come prepared for this meeting, and from the front pocket of his pack he pulled out his wallet and handed a coloured snapshot to the guerrilla leader.

In the photograph two men sat on the hood of an ancient Land-Rover. They had their arms around each other's shoulders, and both of them were laughing. Each of them held a beer can in his free hand and with it was saluting the photographer. The accord and camaraderie between them was evident.

The scarred guerrilla studied it for a long time and then slipped the selector on his rifle to lock. "It is Comrade Tungata," he said, and handed the photograph to the others.

"Perhaps," conceded the youngster reluctantly, "but a long time ago. I still think we should shoot him." However, this opinion was now more wistful than determined.

"Comrade Tungata would swallow you without chewing," his companion told him flatly, and slung his rifle over his shoulder.

Craig picked up his leg and in a moment had fitted it to the stump—and instantly all three guerrillas were intrigued, their murderous intentions set aside as they crowded around Craig to examine this marvellous appendage.

Fully aware of the African love of a good joke, Craig clowned for them. He danced a jig, pirouetted on the leg, cracked himself across the shin without flinching, and finally took the hat of the youngest, most murderous guerrilla from his head, screwed it into a ball and with a cry of "Pele!" drop-kicked it into the lower branches of the wild fig with the artificial leg. The other two hooted with glee, and laughed until tears ran down their cheeks at the youngster's loss of dignity as he scrambled up into the wild fig to retrieve his hat.

Judging the mood finely, Craig opened his pack and brought out mug and whisky bottle. He poured a generous dram and handed the mug to the scar-faced leader.

"Between brothers," he said.

The guerrilla leaned his rifle against the trunk of the tree and accepted the mug. He drained it at one swallow, and blew the fumes ecstatically out of his nose and mouth. The other two took their turn at the mug with as much gusto.

When Craig pulled on his trousers and sat down on his pack, placing the bottle in front of him, they all laid their weapons aside and squatted in a half circle facing him.

"My name is Craig Mellow," he said.

"We will call you Kuphela," the leader told him, "for the leg walks on its own." The others clapped their hands in approbation, and Craig poured each of them a whisky to celebrate his christening.

"My name is Comrade Lookout," the leader told him. Most of the guerrillas had adopted *noms-de-guerre.* "This is Comrade Peking." A tribute to his Chinese instructors, Craig guessed. "And this," the leader indicated the youngest, "is Comrade Dollar." Craig had difficulty remaining straight-faced at this unlikely juxtaposition of ideologies.

"Comrade Lookout," Craig said, "the *kanka* marked you."

The *kanka* were the jackals, the security forces, and Craig guessed the leader would be proud of his battle scars.

Comrade Lookout caressed his cheek. "A bayonet. They thought I was dead and they left me for the hyena."

"Your leg?" Dollar asked in return. "From the war also?"

An affirmative would tell them that he had fought against them. Their reaction was unpredictable, but Craig paused only a second before he nodded. "I trod on one of our own mines."

"Your own mine!" Lookout crowed with delight at the joke. "He stood on his own mine!" And the others thought it as funny, but Craig detected no residual resentment.

"Where?" Peking wanted to know.

"On the river, between Kazungula and Victoria Falls."

"Ah, yes." They nodded at each other. "That was a bad place. We crossed there often," Lookout remembered. "That is where we fought the Scouts."

The Ballantyne Scouts had been one of the elite units of the security forces, and Craig had been attached to them as an armourer.

"The day I trod on the mine was the day the Scouts followed your people across the river. There was a terrible fight on the Zambian side, and all the Scouts were wiped out."

"Hau! Hau!" they exclaimed with amazement. "That was the day! We were there—we fought with Comrade Tungata on that day."

"What a fight—what a fine and beautiful killing when we trapped them," Dollar remembered with the killing light in his eyes again.

"They fought! Mother of Nkulu kulu—how they fought! Those were real men!"

Craig's stomach churned queasily with the memory. His own cousin, Roland Ballantyne, had led the Scouts across the river that fateful day. While Craig lay shattered and bleeding on the edge of the minefield, Roland and all his men had fought to the death a few miles farther on. Their bodies had been abused and desecrated by these men, and now they were discussing it like a memorable football match.

Craig poured more whisky for them. How he had loathed them and their fellows—"terrs," they called them, terrorists—loathed them with the special hatred reserved for something that threatens your very existence and all that you hold dear. But now, in his turn, he saluted them with the mug, and drank. He had heard of R.A.F. and Luftwaffe pilots meeting after the war and reminiscing as they were doing, more like comrades than deadly enemies.

"Where were you when we rocketed the storage tanks in Harare and burned the fuel?" they asked.

"Do you remember when the Scouts jumped from the sky onto our camp at Molingushi? They killed eight hundred of us that day—and I was there!" Peking recalled with pride. "But they did not catch me!"

Yet now Craig found that he could not sustain that hatred any longer. Under the veneer of cruelty and savagery imposed upon them by war, they were the true Matabele that he had always loved, with that irrepressible sense of fun, that deep pride in themselves and their tribe, that abounding sense of personal honour, of loyalty and their own peculiar code of morals. As they chatted, Craig warmed to them, and they sensed it and responded to him in turn.

"So what makes you come here, Kuphela? A sensible man like you, walking without even a stick into the leopard's cave? You must have heard about us—and yet you came here?"

"Yes, I have heard about you. I heard that you were hard men, like old Mzilikazi's warriors."

They preened a little at the compliment.

"But I came here to meet you and talk with you," Craig went on.

"Why?" demanded Lookout.

"I will write a book, and in the book I will write truly the way you are and the things for which you are still fighting."

"A book?" Peking was suspicious immediately.

"What kind of book?" Dollar backed him.

"Who are you to write a book?" Lookout's voice was openly scornful.

"You are too young. Book-writers are great and learned people." Like all barely literate Africans, he had an almost superstitious awe of the printed word, and reverence for the grey hairs of age.

"A one-legged book-writer," Dollar scoffed, and Peking giggled and picked up his rifle. He placed it across his lap and giggled again. The mood had changed once more. "If he lies about this book, then perhaps he lies about his friendship with Comrade Tungata," Dollar suggested with relish.

Craig had prepared for this also. He took a large manila envelope from the flap of his pack and shook from it a thick sheath of newspaper cuttings. He shuffled through them slowly, letting their disbelieving mockery change to interest, then he selected one and handed it to Lookout. The serial of the book had been shown on Zimbabwe television two years previously, before these guerrillas had returned to the bush, and it had enjoyed an avid following throughout its run.

"Hau!" Lookout exclaimed. "It is the old king, Mzilikazi!"

The photograph at the head of the article showed Craig on the set with members of the cast of the production. The guerrillas immediately recognized the black American actor who had taken the part of the old Matabele king. He was in costume of leopard-skin and heron-feathers.

"And that is you—with the king." They had not been as impressed, even by the photograph of Tungata.

There was another cutting, a photo taken in the big Doubleday Book Shop on Fifth Avenue, of Craig standing beside a huge pyramid of the book, with a blow-up of his portrait from the back cover riding atop it.

"That is you!" They were truly stunned now. "Did you write that book?"

"Now do you believe?" Craig demanded, but Lookout studied the evidence carefully before committing himself.

His lips moved as he read slowly through the text of the articles, and when he handed them back to Craig, he said seriously, "Kuphela, despite your youth, you are indeed an important book-writer."

Now they were almost pathetically eager to pour out their grievances to him, like petitioners at a tribal *indaba* where cases were heard and judgement handed down by the elders of the tribe. While they talked, the sun rose up across a sky as blue and unblemished as a heron's egg, and reached its noon and started its stately descent towards its bloody death in the sunset.

What they related was the tragedy of Africa, the barriers that divided this mighty continent and which contained all the seeds of violence and disaster, the single incurable disease that inflicted them all—tribalism.

Here it was Matabele against Mashona.

"The dirt-eaters," Lookout called them, "the lurkers in caves, the fugitives on the fortified hilltops, the jackals who will only bite when your back is turned to them."

It was the scorn of the warrior for the merchant, of the man of direct action for the wily negotiator and politician.

"Since great Mzilikazi first crossed the river Limpopo, the Mashona have been our dogs—*amaholi*, slaves and sons of slaves."

This history of displacement and domination of one group by another was not confined to Zimbabwe, but over the centuries had taken place across the entire continent. Farther north, the lordly Masai had raided and terrorized the Kikuyu who lacked their warlike culture; the giant Watutsi, who considered any man under six feet six to be a dwarf, had taken the gentle Hutu as slaves—and in every case, the slaves had made up for their lack of ferocity with political astuteness, and as soon as the white colonialists' protection was withdrawn, had either massacred their tormentors, as the Hutu had the Watutsi, or had bastardized the doctrine of Westminster government by discarding the checks and balances that make the system equitable, and had used their superior numbers to place their erstwhile masters into a position of political subjugation, as the Kikuyu had the Masai.

Exactly the same process was at work here in Zimbabwe. The white settlers had been rendered inconsequential by the bush war, and the concepts of fair play and integrity that the white administrators and civil servants had imposed upon all the tribes had been swept away with them.

"There are five dirt-eating Mashona for every one Matabele *indoda*," Lookout told Craig bitterly, "but why should that give them any right to lord it over us? Should five slaves dictate to a king? If five baboons bark, must the black-maned lion tremble?"

"That is the way it is done in England and America," Craig said mildly. "The will of the majority must prevail—"

"I piss with great force on the will of the majority," Lookout dismissed the doctrine of democracy airily. "Such things might work in England and America—but this is Africa. They do not work here—I will not bow down to the will of five dirt-eaters. No, not to the will of a hundred, nor a thousand of them. I am Matabele, and only one man dictates to me—a Matabele king."

Yes, Craig thought, this *is* Africa. The old Africa awakening from the trance induced in it by a hundred years of colonialism, and reverting immediately to the old ways.

He thought of the tens of thousands of fresh-faced young Englishmen who for very little financial reward had come out to spend their lives in the Colonial Service, labouring to instil into their reluctant charges their respect for the Protestant work-ethic, the ideal of fair-play and Westminster government—young men who had returned to England prematurely aged and broken in health, to eke out their days on a pittance of a pension and the belief that they had given their lives to something that was valuable and lasting. Did they, Craig wondered, ever suspect that it might all have been in vain?

The borders that the colonial system had set up had been neat and orderly. They followed a river, or the shore of a lake, the spine of a mountain range, and where these did not exist, a white surveyor with a theodolite had shot a line across the wilderness. "This side is German East Africa, this side is British." But they took no cognizance of the tribes that they were splitting in half as they drove in their pegs.

"Many of our people live across the river in South Africa," Peking complained. "If they were with us, then things would be different. There would be more of us, but now we are divided."

"And the Shona is cunning, as cunning as the baboons that come down to raid the maize fields in the night. He knows that one Matabele warrior would eat a hundred of his, so when first we rose against them, he used the white soldiers of Smith's government who had stayed on—"

Craig remembered the delight of the embittered white soldiers who considered they had not been defeated but had been betrayed, when the Mugabe government had turned them loose on the dissenting Matabele faction.

"The white pilots came in their aeroplanes, and the white troops of the Rhodesian Regiment—"

After the fighting the shunting-yards at Bulawayo station had been crowded with refrigerated trucks each packed from floor to roof with the bodies of the Matabele dead.

"The white soldiers did their work for them, while Mugabe and his boys ran back to Harare and climbed shaking and snivelling under their women's skirts. Then, after the white soldiers had taken our weapons, they crawled out again, shook off the dust of their retreat, and came strutting back like conquerors."

"They have dishonoured our leaders—"

Nkomo, the Matabele leader, had been accused of harbouring rebels and accumulating caches of weapons, and driven in disgrace by Mashona-dominated government into enforced retirement.

"They have secret prisons in the bush where they take our leaders," Peking went on. "There they do things to our men that do not bear talking of.

"Now that we are deprived of weapons, their special units move through the villages. They beat our old men and women, they rape our young women, they take our young men away, never to be seen or heard of again."

Craig had seen a photograph of men in the blue and khaki of the former British South Africa police, so long the uniform of honour and fair play, carrying out interrogations in the villages. In the photograph they had a naked Matabele spread-eagled on the earth, an armed and uniformed constable standing with both booted feet and his full weight on each ankle and wrist to pin him, while two other constables wielded clubs as heavy as baseball bats. They were using full strokes from high above the head, and raining blows on the man's back and shoulders and buttocks. The photograph had been captioned "Zimbabwe Police interrogate suspect in attempt to learn whereabouts of American and British tourists abducted as hostages by Matabele dissidents." There had been no photographs of what they did to the Matabele girls.

"Perhaps the government troops were looking for the hostages which you admit you seized," Craig pointed out tartly. "A little while ago you would have been quite happy to kill me or take me hostage as well."

"The Shona began this business long before we took our first hostage," Lookout shot back at him.

"But you *are* taking innocent hostages," Craig insisted. "Shooting white farmers—"

"What else can we do to make people understand what is happening to our people? We have very few leaders who have not been imprisoned or silenced, and even they are powerless. We have no weapons except these few we have managed to hide, we have no powerful friends, while the Shona have Chinese and British and American allies. We have no money to continue the struggle—and they have all the wealth of the land and millions of dollars of aid from these powerful friends. What else can we do to make the world understand what is happening to us?"

Craig decided prudently that this was neither the time nor the place to offer a lecture on political morality—and then he thought wryly,

"Perhaps my morality is old-fashioned, anyway." There was a new political expediency in international affairs that had become acceptable: the right of impotent and voiceless minorities to draw violent attention to their own plight. From the Palestinians and the Basque separatists to the bombers of Northern Ireland blowing young British guardsmen and horses to bloody tatters in a London street, there was an odd, new morality abroad. With these examples before them, and from their own experience of successfully bringing about political change by violence, these young men were children of the new morality.

Though Craig could never bring himself to condone these methods, not if he lived a hundred years, yet he found himself in grudging sympathy with their plight and their aspirations. There had always been a strange and sometimes bloody bond between Craig's family and the Matabele. A tradition of respect and understanding for a people who were fine friends and enemies to be wary of, an aristocratic, proud and warlike race that deserved better than they were now receiving.

There was an elitist streak in Craig's make-up that hated to see a Gulliver rendered impotent by Lilliputians. He loathed the politics of envy and the viciousness of socialism which, he felt, sought to strike down the heroes and reduce every exceptional man to the common greyness of the pack, to replace true leadership with the oafish mumblings of trade-union louts, to emasculate all initiative by punitive tax schemes and then gradually to shepherd a numbed and compliant populace into the barbed-wire enclosure of Marxist totalitarianism.

These men were terrorists—certainly. Craig grinned. Robin Hood was also a terrorist—but at least he had some style and a little class.

"Will you see Comrade Tungata?" they demanded with almost pitiful eagerness.

"Yes. I will see him soon."

"Tell him we are here. Tell him we are ready and waiting."

Craig nodded. "I will tell him."

They walked back with him to where he had left the Volkswagen, and Comrade Dollar insisted on carrying Craig's pack. When they reached the dusty and slightly battered VW, they piled into it with AK 47 barrels protruding from three windows.

"We will go with you," Lookout explained, "as far as the main Victoria Falls Road, for if you should meet another of our patrols when you are alone, it might go hard for you."

They reached the macadamized Great North Road well after night had fallen. Craig stripped his pack and gave them what remained of his rations and the dregs of the whisky. He had two hundred dollars in his wallet and he added that to the booty. Then they shook hands.

"Tell Comrade Tungata we need weapons," said Dollar.

"Tell him that, more than weapons, we need a leader." Comrade Lookout gave Craig the special grip of thumb and palm reserved for trusted friends. "Go in peace, Kuphela," he said. "May the leg that walks alone carry you far and swiftly."

"Stay in peace, my friend," Craig told him.

"No, Kuphela, rather wish me bloody war!" Lookout's scarred visage twisted into a dreadful grin in the reflected headlights.

When Craig looked back, they had disappeared into the darkness as silently as hunting leopards.

* * *

"I wouldn't have taken any bets on seeing you again," Jock Daniels greeted Craig when he walked into the auctioneer's office the next morning. "Did you make it up to the Chizarira—or did good sense get the better of you?"

"I'm still alive, aren't I?" Craig evaded the direct question.

Jock nodded. "Good boy. No sense messing with those Matabele *shufta*—bandits the lot of them."

"Did you hear from Zürich?"

Jock shook his head. "Only sent the telex at nine o'clock local time. They are an hour behind us."

"Can I use your telephone? A few private calls?"

"Local? I don't want you chatting up your birds in New York at my expense."

"Of course."

"Right—as long as you mind the shop for me, while I'm out."

Craig installed himself at Jock's desk and consulted the cryptic notes that he had made from Henry Pickering's file.

His first call was to the American Embassy in Harare, the capital three hundred miles north-east of Bulawayo.

"Mr. Morgan Oxford, your cultural attaché, please," he asked the operator.

"Oxford." The accent was crisp Boston and Ivy League.

"Craig Mellow. A mutual friend asked me to call you and give you his regards."

"Yes, I was expecting you. Won't you come in here any time and say hello?"

"I'd enjoy that," Craig told him, and hung up.

Henry Pickering was as good as his word. Any message handed to Oxford would go out in the diplomatic bag and be on Pickering's desk within twelve hours.

His next call was to the office of the minister of tourism and information, and he finally got through to the minister's secretary. Her attitude changed to warm co-operation when he spoke to her in Sindebele.

"The comrade minister is in Harare for the sitting of Parliament," she told him, and gave Craig his private number at the House.

Craig got through to a parliamentary secretary on his fourth attempt. The telephone system had slowly begun deteriorating, he noticed. The blight of all developing countries was lack of skilled artisans; prior to independence all linesmen had been white, and since then most of them had taken the gap.

This secretary was Mashona and insisted on speaking English as proof of her sophistication.

"Kindly state the nature of the business to be discussed." She was obviously reading from a printed form.

"Personal. I am acquainted with the comrade minister."

"Ah yes. P-e-r-s-o-n-n-e-l." The secretary spelled it out laboriously as she wrote it.

"No—that's p-e-r-s-o-n-a-l," Craig corrected her patiently. He was beginning to adjust to the pace of Africa again.

"I will consult the comrade minister's schedule. You will be obliged to telephone again."

Craig consulted his list. Next was the government registrar of companies, and this time he was lucky. He was put through to an efficient and helpful clerk who made a note of his requirements.

"The Share Register, Articles and Memorandum of Association of the company trading as Rholands Ltd., formerly known as Rhodesian Lands and Mining Ltd." He heard the disapproval in the clerk's tone of voice. "Rhodesian" was a dirty word nowadays, and Craig made a mental resolution to change the company's name, if ever he had the power to do so. "Zimlands" would sound a lot better to an African ear.

"I will have roneoed copies ready for you to collect by four o'clock," the clerk assured him. "The search fee will be fifteen dollars."

Craig's next call was to the surveyor general's office, and again he arranged for copies of documents—this time the titles to the company properties—the ranches King's Lynn, Queen's Lynn and the Chizarira estates.

Then there were fourteen other names on his list, all of whom ranching in Matabeleland when he left, close neighbours and friends of his family, those that grandpa Bawu had trusted and liked.

Of the fourteen he could contact only four, the others had all sold up and taken the long road southward. The remaining families sounded genuinely pleased to hear from him. "Welcome back, Craig. We have all read the book and watched it on TV." But they clammed up immediately he started asking questions. "Damned telephone leaks like a sieve," said one of them. "Come out to the ranch for dinner. Stay the night. Always a bed for you, Craig. Lord knows, there aren't so many of the old faces around any more."

Jock Daniels returned in the middle of the afternoon, red-faced and sweating. "Still burning up my telephone?" he growled. "Wonder if the bottle store has another bottle of that Haig."

Craig responded to this subtlety by crossing the road and bringing back a pinch bottle in a brown paper bag.

"I forgot that you have to have a cast-iron liver to live in this country." He unscrewed the cap and dropped it into the waste-paper basket.

At ten minutes to five o'clock he telephoned the minister's parliamentary office again.

"The Comrade Minister Tungata Zebiwe has graciously consented to meet you at ten o'clock on Friday morning. He can allow you twenty minutes."

"Please convey my sincere thanks to the minister."

That gave Craig three days to kill and meant he would have to drive the three hundred miles to Harare.

"No reply from Zürich?" He sweetened Jock's glass.

"If you made me an offer like that, I wouldn't bother to answer either," Jock grumped, as he took the bottle from Craig's hand and added a little more to the glass.

Over the next few days Craig availed himself of the invitations to visit Bawu's old friends and was smothered with traditional old Rhodesian hospitality.

"Of course, you can't get all the luxuries—Crosse and Blackwell jams, or Bronnley soap—any more," one of his hostesses explained as she piled his plate with rich fare, "but somehow it's fun making do." And she signalled the white-robed table servant to refill the silver dish with baked sweet potatoes.

He spent the days with tanned, slow-speaking men in wide-brimmed felt hats and short khaki trousers, examining their sleek fat cattle from the passenger seat of an open Land-Rover.

"You still can't beat Matabeleland beef," one told him proudly. "Sweetest grass in the whole world. Of course, we have to send it all out through South Africa, but the prices are damned good. Glad I didn't run for it. Heard from old Derek Sanders in New Zealand, working as a hired hand on a sheep station now—and a bloody tough life, too. No Matabele to do the dirty work over there."

He looked at his black herders with paternal affection. "They are just the same, under all the political claptrap. Salt of the bloody earth, my boy. My people, I feel that they are all family, glad I didn't desert them."

"Of course, there are problems," another of his hosts told him. "Foreign exchange is murder—difficult to get tractor spares, and medicine for the stock—but Mugabe's government is starting to wake up. As food-producers we are getting priority on import permits for essentials. Of course, the telephones only work when they do and the trains don't run on time any longer. There is rampant inflation, but the beef prices keep in step with it. They have opened the schools, but we send the kids down south across the border so they get a decent education."

"And the politics?"

"That's between black and black. Matabele and Mashona. The white man's out of it, thank God. Let the bastards tear each other to pieces if they want to. I keep my nose clean, and it's not a bad life—not like the old days, of course, but then it never is, is it?"

"Would you buy more land?"

"Haven't got the money, old boy."

"But if you did have?"

The rancher rubbed his nose thoughtfully. "Perhaps a man could make an absolute mint one day if the country comes right, land prices what they are at the moment—or he could lose the lot if it goes the other way."

"You could say the same of the stock exchange, but in the meantime it's a good life?"

"It's a good life—and, hell, I was weaned on Zambezi waters. I don't reckon I would be happy breathing London smog or swatting flies in the Australian outback."

On Thursday morning Craig drove back to the motel, picked up his laundry, repacked his single canvas hold-all, paid his bill and checked out.

He called at Jock's office. "Still no news from Zürich?"

"Telex came in an hour ago." Jock handed him the flimsy, and Craig scanned it swiftly.

"Will grant your client thirty-day option to purchase all Rholands Company paid-up shares for one half million U.S. dollars payable Zürich in full on signature. No further offers countenanced." They did not come more final than that. Bawu had said double your estimate, and so far he had it right.

Jock was watching his face. "Double your original offer," he pointed out. "Can you swing half a million?"

"I'll have to talk to my rich uncle," Craig teased him. "And anyway I've got thirty days. I'll be back before then."

"Where can I reach you?" Jock asked.

"Don't call me. I'll call you."

He begged another tankful from Jock's private stock and took the Volkswagen out on the road to the north-east, towards Mashonaland and Harare and ran into the first road-block ten miles out of town.

"Almost like the old days," he thought, as he climbed down onto the verge. Two black troopers in camouflage battle-jackets searched the Volkswagen for weapons with painstaking deliberation, while a lieutenant with the cap-badge of the Korean-trained Third Brigade examined his passport.

Once again Craig rejoiced in the family tradition whereby all the expectant mothers in his family, on both the Mellow and the Ballantyne side, had been sent home to England for the event. That little blue booklet with the gold lion and unicorn and *Honi soit qui mal y pense* printed on the cover still demanded a certain deference even at a Third Brigade road-block.

It was late afternoon when he crested the line of low hills and looked down on the little huddle of skyscrapers that rose so incongruously out of the African veld, headstones to the belief in the immortality of the British Empire.

The city that had once borne the name of Lord Salisbury, the foreign secretary who had negotiated the Royal Charter of the British South Africa Company, had reverted to the name Harare after the original Shona chieftain whose cluster of mud and thatch huts the white pioneers had found on the site in September 1890 when they finally completed the long trek up from the south. The streets also had changed their names from those commemorating the white pioneers and Victo-

ria's empire to those of the sons of the black revolution and its allies—
"a street by any other name"—Craig resigned himself.

Once he entered the city he found there was a boom-town atmo-
sphere. The pavements were thronged with noisy black crowds, and the
foyer of the modern sixteen-storied Monomatapa Hotel resounded to
twenty different languages and accents, as tourists jostled visiting bank-
ers and businessmen, foreign dignitaries, civil servants and military advisers.

There was no vacancy for Craig until he spoke to an assistant man-
ager who had seen the TV production and read the book. Then Craig
was ushered up to a room on the fifteenth floor with a view over the
park. While he was in his bath, a procession of waiters arrived bearing
flowers and baskets of fruit and a complimentary bottle of South African champagne. He worked until after midnight on his report to Henry
Pickering and was at the parliament buildings in Causeway by nine-
thirty the next morning.

The minister's secretary kept him waiting for forty-five minutes before leading him through into the panelled office beyond, and Comrade
Minister Tungata Zebiwe stood up from his desk.

Craig had forgotten how powerful was this man's presence, or perhaps he had grown in stature since their last meeting. When he remembered that once Tungata had been his servant, his gunboy, when Craig
was a ranger in the Department of Game Conservation, it seemed that
it had been a different existence. In those days he had been Samson
Kumalo, for Kumalo was the royal blood-line of the Matabele kings,
and he was their direct descendant. Bazo, his great-grandfather, had
been the leader of the Matabele rebellion of 1896 and had been hanged
by the settlers for his part in it. His great-great-grandfather, Gandang,
had been half-brother to Lobengula, the last king of the Matabele
whom Rhodes' troopers had ridden to an ignoble death and unmarked
grave in the northern wilderness after destroying his capital at GuBu-
lawayo, the place of killing.

Royal were his blood-lines, and kingly still his bearing. Taller than
Craig, well over six feet and lean, not yet running to flesh, which was
often the Matabele trait, his physique was set off to perfection by the
cut of his Italian silk suit, shoulders wide as a gallows tree and a flat
greyhound's belly. He had been one of the most successful bush fighters
during the war, and he was warrior still, of that there was no doubt.
Craig experienced a powerful and totally unexpected pleasure in seeing
him once more.

"I see you, Comrade Minister," Craig greeted him, speaking in Sindebele, avoiding having to choose between the old familiar "Sam" and the *nom de guerre* that he now used, Tungata Zebiwe, "the Seeker after Justice."

"I sent you away once," Tungata answered in the same language. "I discharged all debts between us—and sent you away." There was no return light of pleasure in his smoky dark eyes, the heavily boned jaw set hard.

"I am grateful for what you did." Craig was unsmiling also, covering his pleasure. It was Tungata who had signed a special ministerial order allowing Craig to export his self-built yacht *Bawu* from the territory in the face of the rigid exchange-control laws which forbade the removal of even a refrigerator or an iron bedstead. At that time the yacht had been Craig's only possession, and he had still been crippled by the mine blast and confined to a wheelchair.

"I do not want your gratitude," said Tungata, yet there was something behind the burnt-honey-coloured eyes that Craig could not fathom.

"Nor the friendship I still offer you?" Craig asked gently.

"All that died on the battlefield," Tungata said. "It was washed away in blood. You chose to go. Now why have you returned?"

"Because this is my land."

"Your land—" He saw the reddish glaze of anger suffuse the whites of Tungata's eyes. "Your land. You speak like a white settler. Like one of Cecil Rhodes' murdering troopers."

"I did not mean it that way."

"Your people took the land at rifle-point, and at the point of a rifle they surrendered it. Do not speak to me of your land."

"You hate almost as well as you fought," Craig told him, feeling his own anger begin to prickle at the back of his eyes, "but I did not come back to hate. I came back because my heart drew me back. I came back because I felt I could help to rebuild what was destroyed."

Tungata sat down behind his desk and placed his hands upon the white blotter. They were very powerful. He stared at them in a silence that stretched out for many seconds.

"You were at King's Lynn," Tungata broke the silence at last, and Craig started. "Then you went north to the Chizarira."

Craig nodded. "Your eyes are bright. They see all."

"You have asked for copies of the titles to that land." Again Craig was startled, but he remained silent. "But even you must know that you must have government approval to purchase land in Zimbabwe. You must state the use to which you intend to put that land and the capital available to work it."

"Yes, even I know that," Craig agreed.

Tungata looked up at him. "So you come to me to assure me of your friendship. Then, as an old friend, you will ask another favour, is that not so?"

Craig spread his hands, palm upward in a gesture of resignation.

"One white rancher on land that could support five hundred Matabele families. One white rancher growing fat and rich while his servants wear rags and eat the scraps he throws them," Tungata sneered, and Craig shot back at him:

"One white rancher bringing millions of capital into a country starving for it, one white rancher employing dozens of Matabele and feeding and clothing them and educating their children, one white rancher raising enough food to feed ten thousand Matabele, not a mere five hundred. One white rancher cherishing the land, guarding it against goats and droughts, so it will produce for five hundred years, not five—" Craig let his anger boil over and returned Tungata's glare, standing stiff-legged over the desk.

"You are finished here," Tungata growled at him. "The kraal is closed against you. Go back to your boat, your fame and your fawning women, be content that we took only one of your legs—go before you lose your head as well."

Tungata rolled his hand over and glanced at the gold wrist-watch.

"I have nothing more for you," he said, and stood up. Yet, behind his flat, hostile stare, Craig sensed that undefinable thing still there. He tried to fathom it—not fear, he was certain, not guile. A hopelessness, a deep regret, perhaps, even a sense of guilt—or perhaps a blend of many of these things.

"Then, before I go, I have something else for you." Craig stepped closer to the desk and lowered his voice. "You know I was on the Chizarira. I met three men there. Their names were Lookout, Peking and Dollar and they asked me to bring you a message—"

Craig got no further, for Tungata's anger turned to red fury. He was shaking with it, it clouded his gaze and knotted the muscles at the points of his heavy lantern jaw.

"Be silent," he hissed, his voice held low by an iron effort in control. "You meddle in matters that you do not understand, and that do not concern you. Leave this land before they overwhelm you."

Craig returned his gaze defiantly. "I will go, but only after my application to purchase land has been officially denied."

"Then you will leave soon," Tungata replied. "That is my promise to you."

In the parliamentary parking lot the Volkswagen was baking in the morning sun. Craig opened the doors and while he waited for the interior to cool, he found he was trembling with the after-effects of his confrontation with Tungata Zebiwe. He held up one hand before his eyes and watched the tremor of his fingertips. In the Game Department after having hunted down a man-eating lion or a crop-raiding bull elephant, he would have the same adrenalin come-down.

He slipped into the driver's seat, and while he waited to regain control of himself, he tried to arrange his impressions of the meeting and to review what he had learned from it.

Craig had been under surveillance by one of the state intelligence agencies from the moment of his arrival in Matabeleland. Perhaps he had been singled out for attention as a prominent writer—he would probably never know—but his every move had been reported to Tungata.

Yet he could not fathom the true reasons for Tungata's violent opposition to his plans. The reasons he had given were petty and spiteful, and Samson Kumalo had never been either petty or spiteful. Craig was sure that he had sensed correctly that strange mitigating counter-emotion beneath the forbidding reception. There were currents and undercurrents in the deep waters upon which Craig had set sail.

He thought back to Tungata's reaction to his mention of the three dissidents he had met in the wilderness of Chizarira. Obviously Tungata had recognized their names, and his rebuke had been too vicious to have come from a clear conscience. There was much that Craig still wanted to know, and much that Henry Pickering would find interesting.

Craig started the VW and drove slowly back to the Monomatapa down the avenues that had originally been laid out wide enough to enable a thirty-six-ox span to make a U-turn across them.

It was almost noon when he got back to the hotel room. He opened the liquor cabinet and reached for the gin bottle. Then he put it back unopened and rang room service for coffee instead. His daylight drinking habits had followed him from New York, and he knew they had contributed to his lack of purpose. They would change, he decided.

He sat down at the desk at the picture window and gazed down on the billowing blue jacaranda trees in the park while he assembled his thoughts, and then picked up his pen and brought his report to Henry Pickering up to date—including his impressions of Tungata's involvement with the Matabeleland dissidents and his almost guilty opposition to Craig's land-purchase application.

This led logically to his request for financing, and he set out his figures, his assessment of Rholands' potential, and his plans for King's Lynn and Chizarira as favourably as he could. Trading on Henry Pickering's avowed interest in Zimbabwe tourism, he dwelt at length on the development of "Zambezi Waters" as a tourist attraction.

He placed the two sets of papers in separate manila envelopes, sealed them and drove down to the American Embassy. He survived the scrutiny of the marine guard in his armoured cubicle, and waited while Morgan Oxford came through to identify him.

The cultural attaché was a surprise to Craig. He was in his early thirties, as Craig was, but he was built like a college athlete, his hair was cropped short, his eyes were a penetrating blue and his handshake firm, suggesting a great deal more strength than he exerted in his grip.

He led Craig through to a small back office and accepted the two unaddressed manila envelopes without comment.

"I've been asked to introduce you around," he said. "There is a reception and cocktail hour at the French ambassador's residence this evening. A good place to begin. Six to seven—does that sound okay?"

"Fine."

"You staying at the Mono or Meikles?"

"Monomatapa."

"I'll pick you up at 1745 hours."

Craig noted the military expression of time and thought wryly, "Cultural attaché?"

*   *   *

Even under the socialist Mitterand regime, the French managed a characteristic display of *élan*. The reception was on the lawns of the ambassador's residence, with the tricolour undulating gaily on the light evening breeze and the perfume of frangipani blossom creating an illusion of coolness after the crackling heat of the day. The servants were in white ankle-length *kanza* with crimson fez and sash, the champagne, although non-vintage, was Bollinger, and the *foie gras* on the biscuits was from the Périgord. The police band under the spathodea trees at the end of the lawn played light Italian operetta with an exuberant

African beat, and only the motley selection of guests distinguished the gathering from a Rhodesian governor-general's garden party that Craig had attended six years previously.

The Chinese and the Koreans were the most numerous and noticeable, basking in their position of special favour with the government. It was they who had been most constant in aid and material support to the Shona forces during the long bush war, while the Soviets had made a rare error of judgement by courting the Matabele faction, for which the Mugabe government was now making them atone in full measure.

Every group on the lawn seemed to include the squat figures in the rumpled pyjama suits, grinning and bobbing their long lank locks like mandarin dolls, while the Russians formed a small group on their own. Those in uniform were junior officers—there was not even a colonel among them, Craig noted. The Russians could only move upstream from where they were now.

Morgan Oxford introduced Craig to the host and hostess. The ambassadoress was at least thirty years younger than her husband. She wore a bright Pucci print with Parisian chic. Craig said, *"Enchanté, madame,"* and touched the back of her hand with his lips; when he straightened, she gave him a slow speculative appraisal before turning to the next guest in the reception line.

"Pickering warned me you were some kind of cocksman," Morgan chided him gently, "but let's not have a diplomatic incident."

"All right, I'll settle for a glass of bubbly."

Each armed with a champagne flute, they surveyed the lawn. The ladies from the Central African republics were in national dress, a marvellous cacophony of colour like a hatching of forest butterflies, and their men carried elaborately carved walking-sticks or fly-whisks made from animal tails, and the Muslims among them wore embroidered pill-box fezes with the tassel denoting that they were *hadji* who had made the pilgrimage to Mecca.

Craig thought of his grandfather, the arch-colonist. "Sleep well, Bawu. It is best that you never lived to see this."

"We had better check you in with the Brits, seeing that's your home base," Morgan suggested, and introduced him to the British High Commissioner's wife, an iron-jawed lady with a lacquered hair-style modelled on Margaret Thatcher's.

"I can't say I enjoyed all that detailed violence in your book," she told him severely. "Do you think it was really necessary?"

Craig kept any trace of irony out of his voice. "Africa is a violent land. He who would hide that fact from you is no true story-teller." He wasn't really in the mood for amateur literary critics, and he looked past her and rove the lawn, seeking distraction.

What he found made his heart jump against his ribs like a caged animal. From across the lawn she was watching him with green eyes from under that unbroken line of dark thick brows. She wore a cotton skirt with patch-pockets that left her calves bare, open sandals that laced around her ankles and a simple T-shirt. Her thick dark hair was tied with a leather thong at the back of her neck; it was freshly washed and shiny. Although she wore no make-up, her tanned skin had the lustre of abounding health and her lips were rouged with the bright young blood beneath. Over one shoulder was slung a Nikon FM with motor drive and both her hands were thrust into the pockets of her skirt.

She had been watching him, but the moment Craig looked directly at her, she lifted her chin in a gesture of mild disdain, held his eye for just long enough and then turned her head unhurriedly to the man who stood beside her, listening intently to what he was saying and then showing white teeth in a small controlled laugh. The man was an African, almost certainly Mashona, for he wore the crisply starched uniform of the regular Zimbabwean army and the red staff tabs and stars of a brigadier-general. He was as handsome as the young Harry Belafonte.

"Some guys have a good eye for horseflesh," Morgan said softly, mocking again. "Come along, then, I'll introduce you."

Before Craig could protest, he had started across the lawn and Craig had to follow.

"General Peter Fungabera, may I introduce Mr. Craig Mellow. Mr. Mellow is the celebrated novelist."

"How do you do, Mr. Mellow. I apologize for not having read your books. I have so little time for pleasure." His English was excellent, his choice of words precise but strongly accented.

"General Fungabera is Minister of Internal Security, Craig," Morgan explained.

"A difficult portfolio, General." Craig shook his hand, and saw that though his eyes were penetrating and cruel as a falcon's, there was a humorous twist to his smile, and Craig was instantly attracted to him. A hard man, but a good one, he judged.

The general nodded. "But then nothing worth doing is ever easy, not even writing books. Don't you agree, Mr. Mellow?"

He was quick and Craig liked him more, but his heart was still pumping and his mouth was dry so he could concentrate only a small part of his attention on the general.

"And this," said Morgan, "is Miss Sally-Anne Jay." Craig turned to face her. How long ago since he had last done so, a month perhaps? But he found that he remembered clearly every golden fleck in her eyes and every freckle on her cheeks.

"Mr. Mellow and I have met—though I doubt he would remember." She turned back to Morgan and took his arm in a friendly, familiar gesture. "I am so sorry I haven't seen you since I got back from the States, Morgan. Can't thank you enough for arranging the exhibition for me. I have received so many letters—"

"Oh, we've had feedback also," Morgan told her. "All of it excellent. Can we have lunch next week? I'll show you." He turned to explain. "We sent an exhibition of Sally-Anne's photographs on a tour of all our African consular offices. Marvellous stuff, Craig, you really must see her work."

"Oh, he has." Sally-Anne smiled without warmth. "But unfortunately Mr. Mellow does not have your enthusiasm for my humble efforts." And then without giving Craig a chance to protest, she turned back to Morgan. "It's wonderful, General Fungabera has promised to accompany me on a visit to one of the rehabilitation centres, and he will allow me to do a photographic series—" With a subtle inclination of her body she effectively excluded Craig from the conversation, and left him feeling gawky and wordless on the fringe.

A light touch on his upper arm rescued him from embarrassment and General Fungabera drew him aside just far enough to ensure privacy.

"You seem to have a way of making enemies, Mr. Mellow."

"We had a misunderstanding in New York." Craig glanced sideways at Sally-Anne.

"Although I did detect a certain arctic wind blowing there, I was not referring to the charming young photographer, but to others more highly placed and in a better position to render you disservice." Now all Craig's attention focused upon Peter Fungabera as he went on softly, "Your meeting this morning with a cabinet colleague of mine was," he paused, "shall we say, unfruitful?"

"Unfruitful will do very nicely," Craig agreed.

"A great pity, Mr. Mellow. If we are to become self-sufficient in our food supplies and not dependent on our racist neighbours in the south, then we need farmers with capital and determination on land that is now being abused."

"You are well informed, General, and far-seeing." Did everyone in the country already know exactly what he intended? Craig wondered.

"Thank you, Mr. Mellow. Perhaps when you are ready to make your application for land purchase, you will do me the honour of speaking to me again. A friend at court, isn't that the term? My brother-in-law is the Minister for Agriculture."

When he smiled, Peter Fungabera was irresistible. "And now, Mr. Mellow, as you heard, I am going to accompany Miss Jay on a visit to certain closed areas. The international press have been making a lot of play regarding them. Buchenwald, I think one of them wrote, or was it Belsen? It occurs to me that a man of your reputation might be able to set the record straight, a favour for a favour, perhaps—and if you travelled in the same company as Miss Jay, then it might give you an opportunity to sort out your misunderstanding, might it not?"

*   *   *

It was still dark and chilly when Craig parked the Volkswagen in the lot behind one of the hangars at New Sarum air force base and, lugging his hold-all, ducked through the low side-entrance into the cavernous interior.

Peter Fungabera was there ahead of him, talking to two air force non-commissioned officers, but the moment he saw Craig he dismissed them with a casual salute and came towards Craig smiling.

He wore a camouflage battle-jacket and the burgundy-red beret and silver leopard's-head cap-badge of the Third Brigade. Apart from a holstered side-arm, he carried only a leather-covered swagger-stick.

"Good morning, Mr. Mellow. I admire punctuality." He glanced down at Craig's hold-all. "And the ability to travel lightly."

He fell in beside Craig and they went out through the tall rolling doors onto the hardstand.

There were two elderly Canberra bombers parked before the hangar. Now the pride of the Zimbabwe air force, they had once mercilessly blasted the guerrilla camps beyond the Zambezi. Beyond them stood a sleek little silver and blue Cessna 210, and Peter Fungabera headed towards it just as Sally-Anne appeared from under the wing. She was engrossed in her walkaround checks and Craig realized she was to be their pilot. He had expected a helicopter and a military pilot.

She was dressed in a Patagonia wind-breaker, blue jeans and soft leather mosquito boots. Her hair was covered by a silk scarf. She looked professional and competent as she made a visual check of the fuel level in the wing-tanks and then jumped down to the tarmac.

"Good morning, General. Would you like to take the right-hand seat?"

"Shall we put Mr. Mellow up front? I have seen it all before."

"As you wish." She nodded coolly at Craig, "Mr. Mellow," and climbed up into the cockpit. She cleared with the tower and taxied to the holding point, pulled on the hand-brake and murmured, "Too much pork for good Hebrew education causes trouble."

As a conversational starter it took some following. Craig was dumb-founded, but she ignored him and only when her hands began to dart over the controls setting the trim, checking masters, mags and mixture, pushing the pitch fully fine, did he understand that the phrase was her personal acronym for the pre-take-off check-list, and the mild misgivings that he had had about female pilots began to recede.

After take-off, she turned out of the circuit on a north-westerly heading and engaged the automatic pilot, opened a large-scale map on her lap and concentrated on the route. Good flying technique, Craig admitted, but not much for social intercourse.

"A beautiful machine," Craig tried. "Is it your own?"

"Permanent loan from the World Wildlife Trust," she answered, still intent on the sky directly ahead.

"What does she cruise at?"

"There is an air-speed indicator directly in front of you, Mr. Mellow." She crushed him effortlessly.

It was Peter Fungabera who leaned over the back of Craig's seat and ended the silence.

"That's the Great Dyke," he pointed out the abrupt geological formation below them. "A highly mineralized intrusion—chrome, platinum, gold—" Beyond the dyke, the farming lands petered out swiftly and they were over a vast area of rugged hills and sickly green forests that stretched endlessly to a milky horizon.

"We will be landing at a secondary airstrip, just this side of the Pongola Hills. There is a mission station there and a small settlement, but the area is very remote. Transport will meet us there but it's another two hours' drive to the camp," the general explained.

"Do you mind if we go down lower, General?" Sally-Anne asked, and Peter Fungabera chuckled.

"No need to ask the reason. Sally-Anne is educating me in the importance of wild animals, and their conservation."

Sally-Anne eased back the throttle and went down. The heat was building up and the light aircraft began to bounce and wobble as it met the thermals coming up from the rocky hills. The area below them was devoid of human habitation and cultivation.

"God-forsaken hills," the general growled. "No permanent water, sour grazing and fly."

However, Sally-Anne picked out a herd of big beige humpbacked eland in one of the open vleis beside a dry river-bed, and then, twenty miles farther on, a solitary bull elephant.

She dropped to tree-top level, pulled on the flaps and did a series of steep slow turns around the elephant, cutting him off from the forest and holding him in the open, so he was forced to face the circling machine with ears and trunk extended.

"He's magnificent!" she cried, the wind from the open window buffeting them and whipping her words away. "A hundred pounds of ivory each side," and she was shooting single-handed through the open window, the motor drive on her Nikon whirring as it pumped film through the camera.

They were so low that it seemed the bull might grab a wing-tip with his reaching trunk, and Craig could clearly make out the wet exudation from the glands behind his eyes. He found himself gripping the sides of his seat.

At last Sally-Anne left him, levelled her wings and climbed away. Craig slumped with relief.

"Cold feet, Mr. Mellow? Or should that be singular, foot?"

"Bitch," Craig thought. "That was a low hit." But she now was talking to Peter Fungabera over her shoulder.

"Dead, that animal is worth ten thousand dollars, tops. Alive, he's worth ten times that, and he'll sire a hundred bulls to replace him."

"Sally-Anne is convinced that there is a large-scale poaching ring at work in this country. She has shown me some remarkable photographs —and I must say, I am beginning to share her concern."

"We have to find them and smash them, General," she insisted.

"Find them for me, Sally-Anne, and I will smash them. You already have my word."

Listening to them talking, Craig felt again an old-fashioned emotion that he had been aware of the first time he had seen these two together. There was no missing the accord between them, and Fungabera was a dashingly handsome fellow. Now he darted a glance over his shoulder